BACK AGAINST THE WALL

BY

BARBARA BARRETT

A MAH JONGG MYSTERY

Print ISBN: 978-1-948532-81-5

This book is dedicated to Mitzi, Shelby, Ebenezer and Simon, the dogs that have enriched my life.

Chapter One

"Gather round, everyone. You won't believe this," Bitsy Melzer told the other mah jongg players in the room.

Marianne Putnam, always the analyst, wondered what Bitsy was up to today.

The gathering included her three fast friends who she'd met a few years back. The four of them had since helped the sheriff's office in Serendipity Springs, Florida, solve a number of murders: Sydney Bonner, self-appointed leader of the foursome; Micki Demetrius, the freelance journalist whose curiosity frequently embroiled her in scary situations; and Katrina "Kat" Faulkner, cabaret singer turned restaurateur, rancher and multimillionaire following a huge win in a national lottery.

The other eleven guests invited to Bitsy's home gathered round her new automatic mah jongg table, clearly the star of the show. This wasn't some ordinary square table. This one was equipped with two full sets of mah jongg tiles, one waiting inside to be summoned once the one on the tabletop had been played.

Bitsy, almost as short as Marianne's five-one stature, made a production of hitting a button on a circle in the middle of the table, causing the circle to rise about eight inches. "Now push all the tiles into the hole underneath the circle," she said. The women sitting at the table complied, dumping all hundred and forty-four pink-backed tiles into the chasm below.

Bitsy, her pixie-styled hair still coal-black with only a few traces of gray, leaned over one of the women and paused dramatically. "And voilà!" she said as she pushed another button on the circle. The circle now lowered to its initial location, and within a beat, four rows of blue-backed tiles rose from below and rested against the four tile racks along the sides. Each row of the new tiles contained nineteen tiles with another row of nineteen stacked on top of it.

"Wow!" Marianne cried, clapping her hands together. "It's ready to go for the next game. We players don't have to do anything except sit back and let the table do its thing." She never knew what to expect with Bitsy, who sometimes exaggerated her news. But this time she'd been right on the money when she claimed she had a fabulous surprise for the group.

"Isn't it something else?" Bitsy wanted to know. "I've been hinting to my husband, Mark, that I wanted one of these things for what seems like months, but I never thought he'd actually get me one. Even for our fortieth anniversary."

"Kudos for Mark," Syd said. "My birthday is coming up in another month. Maybe I can borrow some of your hints to throw Trip's direction."

"What a terrific gift," Kat said. "I can't wait to use it."

"I thought we could take turns trying it out this afternoon," Bitsy told her and the other women. "Each group of four changes tables after every game. I know, we're not used to that routine, but just this once I thought we could give it a go so everyone gets to have fun with it for at least one game."

Micki's hand shot into the air. "Sign me up! Wish I could get one of these for myself, but there's no room for something like this in my small condo."

There would be room when and if Micki decided to move in with Guy Whitney, the man she'd finally let into her heart in the last year. Guy, a retired attorney and widower, owned a beautiful two-story Tudor. But this wasn't the place to remind her friend of that possibility, in front of all these eager witnesses.

Micki wasn't ready to drop the idea. "Why don't you gift the group with a bunch of tables we could use at the community center, Kat?" she asked, unable to refrain from commenting on Kat's recently found wealth from the lottery.

Marianne cut off that idea before Kat had to refuse it. "You've got to stop spending Kat's money for her, Mick. Besides, just like your condo, I doubt there'd be enough room at the community center for four of these tables. I doubt they'd disassemble for easy storage."

Kat shot her a thankful look.

"Hadn't thought about that," Micki admitted with disappointment.

"Maybe we can add one to the ranch house as part of Syd's remodeling efforts?" Kat said, bringing up the project that seemed to have no end. Syd, thinking she needed something to keep her occupied while the other three were off pursuing their individual interests, had decided to take up interior design and begged Kat to let her fix up the aging ranch house Kat had purchased on a whim months ago.

Knowing them as well as she did, Marianne wondered how either of the two women would live through the process. Sweet-tempered Kat wasn't one to be pleased easily. There always seemed to be one more detail to lay on her friend. Like now, offering to add one of these mechanical tile-traders to the house. And Syd wasn't one to have last-minute changes laid on her. Flexibility didn't come easily for such a strong-minded woman.

Fortunately, Syd was preoccupied at the moment studying the table and didn't hear the exchange between Kat and Micki.

For all the time-saving promised by the automatic tile setup, the afternoon went slowly. After each game ended on the new table, the group using it had to wait for the other three tables to finish their game before the rotation could start. No one started up again until all sixteen women watched the "changing of the guard" on the automatic table.

"That was fun," Kat said as the four of them piled into Syd's car.

"Different, anyhow," Syd replied.

"You don't sound all that impressed with the new table," Marianne said to her.

"It was all right," Syd said. "It's just that Bitsy's always trying to one-up us. First it was her fancy new home. Then the latest car her husband bought her. And now it's this table."

Syd liked being the center of attention, just like Micki. Not that either one craved it. They were just accustomed to people and things revolving around them. "Did you ever think that's because she wants to be more a part of things?" Marianne asked.

"By lording over us all her new trinkets?" Syd replied.

"Well, yes," Marianne conceded. "You command everyone else's attention just by being you. Not everyone has that kind of power. Not Bitsy, anyhow."

Kat leaned forward from her seat in the back of the car and touched Marianne's shoulder. "Good call. I sensed something like that was going on with her, but you put it into words."

"You make me sound like an ogre," Syd complained.

"That wasn't my intent. I was just trying to explain her behavior so you wouldn't take such a harsh view of it."

"You're right," Syd said with resignation. "That's probably why she's so active in the Serendipity Springs Women's Club and the Trans," the transitional home for women down on their luck.

"Good girl. I knew you'd come round," Marianne said.

"Why do you always have to be the one who sees the best in people?" Syd asked.

Was that how Syd saw her? As some sort of Goody Two-shoes? That wasn't her, was it? And if it was, wasn't that a good thing? Why was she even concerning herself with these questions?

"Who's up for a quick stop at the coffee shop?" Syd asked.

"Afraid you'll have to count me out," Marianne replied. "I still have homework to do for class tomorrow, plus Mortimer needs a nice, long walk. I barely got him out to do his business yesterday. He needs more exercise than that."

"How's it going with your new pet?" Kat asked.

"Like I've told you all more than once, he's not *my* pet. He belongs to our son Rob, who is currently in Scotland in a special management program, and he couldn't take his little darling with him."

"Oops. Didn't mean to step on your toes. I was just inquiring," Kat said.

Marianne drew in a breath. She shouldn't have snapped at her friend like that. "Sorry, Kat. I took my frustration with that dog out on you. My bad. As you probably picked up, Mortimer and I are still adjusting to each other."

"Where's Beau in all this?" Micki asked. "Isn't he helping?"

"He tries. But Beau never had a dog when he was a kid. Nor has our family ever had a pet, let alone a dog. So most of the responsibility for Mortimer has fallen on me." Truth be told, the friendly beagle was growing on her. Other than his creature needs, like eating, sleeping, relieving himself and the never-ending impulse to move, she enjoyed having him around, dozing at her feet.

"Why did you ever agree to such an arrangement?" Syd asked from the front seat.

Because she and Beau had raised them to be independent men with lives of their own, and that's exactly what both Rob and his older brother, Vince, were. So whenever either of them needed something from her, she was a pushover. "You know how it is with our kids, Syd. It wasn't that long ago that you and Trip found yourselves babysitting your young grandchildren when your daughter and her husband needed to work out some things. I recall a rather messy finger-painting session that had you doing more than one load of laundry."

"Those were children. Not a pet. Especially one that needs so much attention."

"Mortimer is Rob's child," Marianne replied. How had she wound up defending the creature that had stared at her with such irritation just that morning? "Anyway, it's a done deal for now. Thank you all for putting up with my complaints."

"I'm up for a quick snack before dinner," Micki said. "I've absorbed about all I can of this week's lesson."

The four of them were taking a special course on private investigation in order to obtain their PI intern licenses. Within the last six months, Kat's fiancé, former sheriff Rick Formero, had set up his own PI business following his defeat at the polls by a snake of an officer who had been involved in a gambling ring. Ironically, Rick's opponent had been killed shortly after taking office, and Rick had been brought in to consult with the interim sheriff, who used to report to him.

Though he could have decided to run again in the next election, Rick, with Kat's blessing, had decided to go private instead. Kat and her three friends and their significant others all wanted to be part of it, having picked up the investigative bug after helping solve nine murders in the last few years.

Since none of them had any formal law enforcement training, they'd have to take the intern route to gain their PI license. Although that required 40 hours of formal training, Micki and Guy had been able to work out a specialized training plan for the four women, Trip Bonner and Beau Putnam approved by the state board. Guy preferred to contribute his legal knowledge and skills from the sidelines.

Marianne, the scientist of the group, who'd been a pharmacist in an earlier career, found the material fascinating, although the personal contact with "suspects" part, volunteers who played the part of suspects, challenged her. Not that she had difficulty talking to people. Just the opposite. Despite her analytical bent, she was a people person. It was so easy for her to get sidetracked in her interviews when the interviewee would tell her something much more fascinating than the case at hand.

"I've finished reading the chapters and need an hour or so yet tonight to review them," she told the other three.

"I finished last week," Syd said.

Though Marianne loved her friend dearly, Syd had a way of making the rest of them feel less than intelligent with her comments about her own study abilities. She'd gone back and forth in her mind whether Syd realized how irritating her comments could be. Especially to Micki, who was struggling. Micki, who seemed to spot conspiracies, wrongdoing and fraud before anyone else, spent more of her time questioning the accuracy of the material than absorbing it.

"As much as I want to become a PI, I continue to question whether all this classroom learning is worth our time," Micki said. "Most of what we've studied thus far has come up in one way or another while we've helped the sheriff's office solve not one or two but a whole bunch of homicides."

"You're the one who, along with Guy, put this whole strategy together for us to fast-track getting our intern designations," Marianne reminded her.

"Guy spearheaded that effort. Then he turned around and decided he didn't need the designation because he could always fall back on his legal training as long as he kept up his CEUs," Micki replied.

"Just a couple more months to go," Kat said. "Then the six of us can officially be part of Formero Investigations."

"That's what you're looking forward to?" Syd asked

incredulously. "What about the rehabbing of your ranch house and then the little matter of your wedding?"

"I haven't forgotten about either, Syd. But at the moment, qualifying for this internship is the one thing I can get my arms around."

Marianne chuckled inwardly. What Kat meant was that the internship was the one thing she could control. Syd seemed to think she was in charge of the reno project, although she was only the designer. Not the owner. And the wedding? Kat and Rick wanted simple. They would have been married months ago if they'd had their way. But their nuptials had somehow become a group project, thanks to Syd and Micki. Syd insisted the event take place at the ranch house, which was still a project in process. And Micki was determined to be wedding planner extraordinaire, choosing not only the bride's gown but also those of her wedding party, i.e., the three of them. She'd also taken over most of the details of the reception, those that didn't compete with Syd's layout.

Marianne was playing her own part managing the guest list and catering, including the cake. Micki insisted on designing the invites.

Kat was just too nice to tell any of them to mind their own business and let her plan her own wedding. And she was the only one of the four who'd never been married. She really should be enjoying all the details.

And Rick was so busy getting his new business off the ground, he hardly noticed what they were all up to.

"How's Rick doing these days?" she asked Kat, although she anticipated hearing the same answer Kat had given them for weeks: Rick was dealing with the challenges of running his own business as well as adapting to no longer being in charge of all the county's law enforcement endeavors. Kat always gave a positive response to the question and was fully committed to helping her man succeed at whatever he chose to do.

"I'm sensing a new undercurrent in his attitude about this new venture the closer we all get to gaining our licenses," Kat said.

"Regret at bringing us on board?" Micki asked.

"No, he's looking forward to us all joining him. But I think the realization that his staff will be made up mostly of his friends and contemporaries is sinking in."

"He's worried about having a team of aging seniors?" Syd asked, cutting to the chase.

"Not worried. I hope I haven't said too much. But we are all discovering limitations we never experienced before as we get older. At least I am. Perhaps that explains why this course is proving to be harder than I thought it would be."

"And those changes could play out in our investigations?" Marianne said, following up on Kat's suggestion.

"I don't disagree," Syd said over her shoulder. "But I say it's too soon to worry about things that haven't happened yet, which when they do, we probably won't be able to stop anyhow."

"You're right," Kat said. "We'll tackle that one if and when it shows up. Getting our internship designations is more than enough."

Chapter Two

ortimer was waiting for Marianne when she got home. Although he hadn't learned how to retrieve his leash from the counter above him, his prancing around said it all. "Where have you been?" Marianne could almost hear him ask.

Beau entered the kitchen from the living room. "Oh, good. You're back just in time to take the dog out."

"Looks like it's past time," she replied as she attached the leash to collar of the white dog covered with large patches of brown and black. "Why didn't you take him?"

"I would have if you'd been much longer. But he seems to prefer you more than me."

True, although the dog still hadn't warmed up to her that much either. Mortimer and Beau could probably become great friends if Beau would just get over his uneasiness around the dog. His parents had never allowed him to have any kind of pet. She suspected his mother didn't want to deal with all the pet hair in her immaculate home, rest her soul. Marianne resolved mentally she was going to ease the tension between man and dog in the weeks ahead, as much for Beau's sake as Mortimer's.

"Sorry, fella," she told the dog, petting him as soon as the leash was on. "My mah jongg afternoon ran long so we could all take turns on Bitsy's new toy." His nose at the back door, he didn't appear to understand nor care. He had one urgent need on his mind.

Why hadn't Beau taken him out to relieve himself? He could at least do that much to help take care of this animal.

Mortimer barely made it five feet from the house before he did his business. Finished, he glanced back at her. "I like it out here in this Florida sunshine. Let's stay out here a while longer," he seemed to be saying.

"Okay, message received," she told him as she led him out toward the front yard, where he stopped yet again and raised his leg. "Oh, c'mon, you already took care of that. No need for an encore. How about a stroll up the street instead?"

His floppy ears went on alert and his tail wagged excitedly.. In a flash, he'd morphed into Perfect Pet and took his position behind Marianne. She could have sworn she heard him say, "Let's go!"

The pilgrimage up and down the block should have gone smoothly. No one else was out, probably because a lot of neighbors hadn't returned yet from their day jobs. The relative serenity did not go over well with the dog, who apparently was accustomed to a lot more activity around Rob's digs. When he wasn't straining at his leash, he was wandering off-route sniffing at fenceposts, flowers or shrubs. Marianne had to keep pulling him back onto the sidewalk.

But that part of their journey was truly a walk in the park compared with the moment woman and dog were joined by another four-footed friend, which started off a world-class mutual sniffing session.

"Daisy! You're never going to make friends that way," a male voice behind them said.

Marianne turned around to discover they'd been joined by another dog walker and his ward, a golden retriever double the size of Mortimer. Apparently the difference in dog sizes hadn't scared Mortimer any as he returned sniff for sniff.

The voice that had chastised the other dog belonged to a man about her age, if one judged by his head of completely gray hair. He was about the same height as Beau, six feet, and dressed in a white golf shirt, khaki pants and topsiders. "So sorry, ma'am. Daisy saw another dog and dragged me here before I could restrain her."

"Apparently they're not in fight mode," she replied to the stranger. "More like getting to know each other."

"Daisy's been crazy to find new dog friends since I brought her home from the rescue center last month. Even though I'm retired, I've been involved in a project at the learning center that's kept me away from my condo more than I realized would be the case when I adopted her. She's having a difficult time adapting. I've been trying with no success to find a nearby dog park so she can run loose and meet other dogs."

"You're ahead of me there," she said. "My husband, Beau, and I are taking care of this guy for our son while he's out of the country. Dog and sitters are still getting used to each other. Tell me more about this dog park you've been looking for. It sounds like the perfect place for our guy too."

"Good luck. As with-it as this community thinks it is, the idea of providing open spaces for pets that are locked inside all day to get a little exercise doesn't appear to have occurred to anyone. I'm Solomon Ridgedale," he said, extending his hand.

Marianne switched Mortimer's leash to her left hand so she could reciprocate. "Marianne Putnam. My husband and I live in that light yellow bungalow down the street."

"Daisy and I live in Forestdale Condos two blocks over. Our daily walks are taking us farther and farther from home as she gets more familiar with the neighborhood and seems to be needing more and more exercise. I've lost five pounds already."

She'd have to remember that. She was always wanting to shed more weight. Maybe these daily jaunts with Mortimer could prove useful. "As for a dog park, who have you talked to so far? Maybe Beau or I know someone who could help."

"There aren't many dog owners in my building, but I did manage to find two. They both have smaller dogs, so their exercise routines didn't extend beyond a quick bound around the block. Then I went to the town's Parks and Recreation Department. A misnomer. All that guy wanted to do was ensure Daisy had all the proper shots and licenses. He's not even the dogcatcher or animal control."

Marianne hadn't considered those requirements when she and Beau agreed to keep Mortimer. Surely Rob had taken care of all the vaccinations, but she wasn't sure about local licensing requirements. Did a visiting dog need anything like that?

"How about the other town departments? Did you check with them?" she asked.

"Went right to the top, the city council, starting with Councilman Drake Busby. It took a couple trips, but I eventually got his ear. I learned from him that the town didn't have any dog parks."

"Drake Busby? I don't think I know him, although if he plays golf, Beau might have heard of him," she replied.

"Busby thought he could get another council member, Porter McHugh, interested, but so far he's met resistance from two of the other three members. Nonetheless, we started working on a proposal to build one."

Marianne couldn't place Porter McHugh either. Had she been so wrapped up in her private investigator course, she'd lost touch with what was happening in the rest of the community? She had very little knowledge of the town's governmental structure other than what had been going on in the sheriff's department the last few years thanks to Kat's involvement with Rick when he was sheriff. And that was with the county, wasn't it?

"Resistance?" she asked. "Why would anyone be opposed to something like a dog park?"

"Why, you ask?" he replied, his tone becoming more animated. "Too much to go into here on a city street. I'd invite you to coffee, but I don't think our dogs would be happy being tied up outside the coffee shop."

Was this some new pickup line? She'd been out of the dating game so long, she doubted she'd recognize one if actually confronted with one. "Why not come to my house? You can go into your story for both me and Beau. Earlier today I made some chocolate chip cookies we can enjoy with our coffee. And the dogs can play outside in the yard while we talk." She'd added the part about Beau just in case this guy had other ideas. *Don't flatter yourself, Marianne!*

They unleased the dogs in her backyard before she took

Solomon in through her back door. From the sounds of the TV coming from the den, Marianne surmised Beau was in there watching a sporting event of some sort when she and Solomon Ridgedale walked into the Putnam house through the back door. "Beau? Can you come out here? There's someone I want you to meet," she called while leading Solomon into the living room, indicating he should make himself comfortable in the easy chair facing the sofa.

She introduced the two men and then excused herself long enough to make coffee and put a plate of cookies together.

"Solomon Ridgedale? I've heard that name somewhere recently," she heard Beau say.

She couldn't hear the rest of the exchange, so she hurriedly got the coffee going and gathered the cookies and napkins. Men had a way of measuring each other up while they compared mutual acquaintances. She didn't want to miss out.

"We've just discovered we both know Trip Bonner," Beau told her when she rejoined them. "He's heard of the follies show Trip produced for the Men's Club a few years back."

Trip had conned her husband, his best friend, into helping with that extravaganza. Beau was still remembering it all as Trip's brilliant success even though Trip's nerves got to him in the end and Syd wound up taking charge of the show. "You were there?" she asked Solomon.

"Oh, no. I only came to town eighteen months ago. After my wife died of cancer, I relocated here from Lancaster, Pennsylvania. We don't have any children, so I was striking out on my own. Took me another year to decide I needed a pet. Before I did that, I joined the Men's Club, although I've learned Trip Bonner more or less dropped out of the group after the Follies."

Dropped out? Maybe that's how some saw it. In reality, he and Syd plus Marianne and Beau, Micki and Guy, and Kat had gotten more involved in solving homicides that seemed to keep popping up since then. But Solomon didn't need to know about that. At least not yet. They hardly knew the man. She'd surprised herself by taking pity on him and inviting him back to the house. He'd seemed so talkative on the sidewalk, and not just because his dog was introducing herself to Mortimer. But now that he was here in her living room chatting with Beau, she wondered if she'd overreacted to his plight.

"Has Solomon told you about our mutual problem yet?" she asked Beau.

Beau offered a perplexed expression. "Mutual problem?"

"We're both dog owners," Solomon answered. "Well, I am, and you two are dog sitters. But all three of us want our babies to be happy, and they're not. My Daisy needs to run off her seemingly boundless energy every day. Your Mortimer appears to be one of those types of dogs that is constantly in motion. Apparently daily walks aren't enough. What they need is to spend time in a dog park releasing all that pent-up vigor and socializing with other dogs. But this town—though I continue to hear from residents what a great place this is to live—has failed to take note of the needs of its dog owners and their pets."

"Serendipity Springs doesn't have a dog park?" Beau said. "I can't believe that. The town is so progressive."

"You'd think, wouldn't you?" Solomon said. He recounted the actions he'd taken to track one down, including talking to

Councilman Busby. "After I finally convinced him to support the idea, I've been helping him put together a proposal to come before the council. He got Councilman Porter McHugh to come on board, but all they've met is resistance from the other three council members. Well, two of them, Tad Brewster and Dan Sheridan. The third, Avery Wallace, the only woman on the council, seems to think she's the peacekeeper since she's the swing vote. Thus far, she hasn't been convinced a dog park is necessary, although I think with enough factual information she could be convinced to change her mind."

"Gift her with her own puppy," Marianne joked.

"Yeah, not that I haven't thought about it," Solomon said, "but when she changes her position, it needs to be solid."

Tad Brewster and Dan Sheridan, two more new names. "Why? Why did those two pooh-pooh it?" she asked.

"Brewster usually objected to further discussion about a dog park because he claimed it hadn't risen to the level of public concern. Busby and McHugh, thinking it would be a no-brainer, hadn't gotten their act together, so they backed down when Brewster demanded to know what evidence they had. The next time they brought it up, they'd done a survey of citizens, and their numbers were impressive. Brewster then switched to another tactic, cost. Busby was ready for this one. He'd done a preliminary budget, which mainly considered the cost of fencing, initial clean-up and layout and then continued maintenance. In response, Brewster hit him with what he must have thought was the coup de grâce, the land it would require. His point, of course, the huge cost to the community to purchase a plot of land."

"Okay, we're with you so far," she said. "And Busby didn't have a rejoinder to that?"

"Actually," Solomon continued, "Busby anticipated that part as well. Apparently he and McHugh researched various locations around town for months. This town has grown to the point where there are no longer that many plots of open land available. Every time they thought they'd found one, either some developer swooped in and bought it for their own purposes or access was limited by one-way streets. Finally, they thought they'd discovered the perfect location, a parcel of city-owned land on the outskirts of town but still within town limits. It was made to be a dog park. Virtually flat with very few trees or other flora that would have to be mowed under. And there'd be room for parking."

"Did Brewster object to that?" she asked.

"Although he thought he'd finally filled in all the blanks, Busby hadn't planned on one last sticking point. The Kerimides Funeral Home."

"A funeral home? That's mainly dead people. Why would they complain about a dog park?" Beau asked.

"True, they wouldn't, but their friends and relatives might not appreciate the noise while attending their somber funerals. At least, that's what the owner and chief mortician, Gordon Kerimides, claimed."

Marianne attempted to take that in. "Really? Yes, I guess barking dogs can disturb the peace at times, but would dogs enjoying the chance to run free and play with other dogs bark that much? Especially if they were behind a fence?"

"I agree," Solomon replied. "However, apparently Kerimides is friends with Brewster."

"That's what it came down to?" Marianne said, incredulous. "Personal relationships? Is the other naysayer, Sheridan, aware of that? Or Avery Wallace?"

"Apparently it's one of those topics they prefer to avoid. Brewster is in charge of issuing mortgages at the bank, which gives him a lot of pull in town beyond his position on the council."

"How about the other naysayer you mentioned?" Beau asked. "What's his objection to the dog park?"

"Dan Sheridan? Busby thinks it's because he wants to stay on the bank's good side. He's developing a new condo complex that's been struggling due to the increased cost of lumber and other building supplies. If he hasn't already sought out more funding from the bank, he probably will in the near future."

Marianne's blood was boiling. She set her coffee cup down on the coffee table before her physical reaction to this discussion caused her to spill. "Personal relationships. Business needs. I hate how things like that influence the greater good of a community," she said.

"Unfortunately, they're what make the world go round, my dear," Beau told her. "Those of us who actually are pulling for the greater good have to recognize that reality and then find the best ways to either combat it or go around it."

"That's so ... unfair!" she replied, surprising herself with the vehemence of her response.

"I don't disagree," Beau said. "But whether we like it or not, it's a reality." He turned back to Solomon. "I assume you've already come to that conclusion?"

Solomon nodded.

"What's your next step? I hope it's not convincing us to sign on to your cause? We certainly support the idea, but we've both got our hands full these days." Beau went on to describe their mission to become private investigator interns and the intense course of study they were following to get there.

"Private investigators? That's great!" Solomon said, his eyes lighting up. "That's what Busby and I need. Somebody to dig up whatever negative background they can find on Brewster. Kerimides, too."

Marianne exchanged a look with Beau. This conversation had left the comfort zone. "Sorry, Solomon. Like Beau said, our time is devoted to completing our course right now. It wouldn't be appropriate for us to accept a project until we've earned our certificate. And even then, as interns we'll be limited in the types of investigations we can accept. However, Rick Formero, who's in charge of Formero Investigations, might consider taking you on."

"He's the one who was beaten at the polls last year, right?" Solomon asked.

"Ye-es," Beau replied. "But as it turned out, when his opponent was murdered, he helped the interim sheriff identify the killer. He's since gone into private practice."

"I'll, uh, consider contacting him." He didn't sound convinced. "I doubt Busby would want to pay for his services for fear his digging for dirt would ever be revealed. And on my own, I'm not sure I could afford Formero."

In other words, Solomon was only interested if he could get free help. But since Rick was still attempting to build his business, it wouldn't hurt to send even a comp case his way. "Just give him a call," she said. "He might offer some suggestions free of charge."

Solomon cocked his head. "Uh, thanks. I'll give it some

thought. Thanks for the coffee and hearing me out. I'd better rescue your backyard from Daisy." With that, he was out the back door in seconds.

"Good for you," Beau told her once it was just the two of them. "At one point, I was afraid you'd agree to help him."

"I came close until I realized I'd invited a complete stranger into our home. A man I'd just met on the street. Although I liked the idea of a dog park, I decided we needed to know more about him before we got any more involved than we already were."

Beau showed his appreciation by pulling her into his arms and hugging her tight. "You did good."

"As much as I've been struggling with our coursework, maybe I have learned a thing or two about smart investigation. One doesn't jump into a case without a little background on their potential client."

Chapter Three

"How was mah jongg today? You met at Bitsy Melzer's place, right? Not at the community center like usual?" Rick asked Kat when she arrived at the McMansion she and Rick had been sharing.

"I spent the bulk of my time watching the others play on Bitsy's new automatic mah jongg table. It shuffles and assembles the tiles for you. Doesn't sound like such a big deal, but it was fascinating to watch the tiles disappear inside the machine and a second set reappear already set up."

Lifting a brow, Rick stared back at her. "That's what gets your motor running? Not an audience to sing for or a new murder case to solve?"

"Those, too, although neither has been in my life lately. I have to get my kicks from little things like mah jongg tiles that get set up hands-free."

He returned that lascivious look he saved only for her. "I thought giving you kicks was my job, Katrina Faulkner."

She moved closer to her fiancé, ran a hand lightly down his forearm. "Of course it is. But we've both been so busy lately, you getting your business set up and me attempting to keep my friends from overdoing their plans for our wedding, we haven't had much opportunity for you-and-me time."

He narrowed his eyes. "Have you felt neglected?"

She squeezed his hand. "Oh, no, Rick. I would've said something. But I have felt overwhelmed a few times. Not by you. By our situations. I just want to be married and settled down with you as my husband. I want the ranch house to be finished and Syd engaged in a project that isn't on my property and not constantly second-guessing my needs."

He took her upper arms in his hands and studied her. "Is this all too much, Katrina? Just say the word and we'll elope. Or you can fire Syd. Or I'll find another place for my office."

She shook her head, smiling wanly. "None of that is necessary. I was just venting. You're the one person I can share all my thoughts and feelings with."

"I beat out your three friends?" he joked.

"Every time. I just need little breaks like playing with the automatic mah jongg table today to get me through this very active period in my life."

He blew out a breath. "Maybe that's what I should be doing. Setting up my PI business is more challenging than I anticipated."

Although she'd suspected for some time that he was having a more difficult time making the transition from county government to the private sector, this was the first time he'd admitted as much to her. What was prompting this confession?

She pulled out of his embrace and guided him over to the sofa in their living room. "Talk to me."

Rick made a face. "Forget I said that."

"No way! Something is nagging at you. Let me in so I can help, if that's possible."

He folded his hands and stared at them several beats before responding. "Helping Brian figure out who killed his predecessor went a long way toward regaining my previous standing in the community. I could've gone back to being sheriff, but I made a conscious decision to move on from that life. Plus, Brian was already doing a great job. But I guess I wasn't prepared for the type of work I'd get as a private 'individual.'"

"Not as exciting?"

"Well, yeah."

Kat wasn't surprised. Her fiancé was an adrenaline junkie. Every day since she'd met him, she'd worried about his safety, his life. She'd been so relieved when he decided to put law enforcement behind him. He could have retired outright and lived the life of leisure he'd earned. But they both knew that wouldn't have been him. At least not yet. There was still another chapter to write before he took up fishing full-time.

"In other words, you're no longer hunting down criminals and solving murders," she said, putting into words what he'd only implied.

He groaned. Not the kind of sound one in pain makes but instead, the moan of someone who's been caught out. "Okay, I admit it. I miss the challenge of finding clues and piecing together the real story behind half-truths I had to work to extract from unwilling witnesses."

"That will come. You know that. Right now, if I can be blunt, you're realizing the extent of the change you willingly accepted."

Nodding, he took her hand. "You're right. Just feelin' sorry for myself."

"That's allowed. At least between us. We're in a building stage, both of us. You with your business, me with gaining the requisite knowledge and skills to join you someday. A lot of people our age would be planning cruises and writing their memoirs. We've chosen a different path. One that requires a little more patience. We just need to hang in there. Something big is on the horizon."

AFTER THEIR COFFEE klatch in her home, Marianne didn't hear any more from Solomon Ridgedale for the next two weeks. She'd almost forgotten about the need for a dog park because she and Beau were getting better acquainted with Mortimer's needs and idiosyncrasies. Even Beau, once he agreed to accompany woman and dog on their walk around the block a few times, gained enough confidence to take Mortimer out on his own.

Out of the blue, she received a text from Solomon inviting them to a city council meeting the next day.

They're at least going to "consider" putting the dog park proposal on an upcoming agenda. Come see your city council "at work."

"What do you think, Beau? We're in between classes right now. Want to see what happens to the dog park idea?"

"As long as we don't let him suck us into running his campaign for him," Beau replied.

"Do you think he'd really do that?"

"We don't know him well enough to say," he said. "But if you agree to sit there and do nothing, I'm in."

Even though she did agree, that wasn't as easy as she thought it would be once the meeting got underway the following day.

She found her mind wandering during the early part of the proceedings as the council members discussed what appeared to be routine matters. The playwright part of her brain had almost settled on the premise of her next one-act when Beau's sharp elbow nudged her side. "Wake up!" he whispered.

"I'm not asleep," she whispered back. "Just using my time more productively."

Councilman Brewster was on his feet. "We've been through this non-issue more times than I wish to recall. Even with Councilman Busby's so-called evidence of a need for such an extravagance, his suggested location does not rise to the level of warranting our attention on a future agenda."

"Rise to the level?" Busby repeated, his volume increasing. "I've already demonstrated the public's desire for a dog park. Now I've found us a no-cost or at least a low-cost solution to making it a reality since it's already public land. The council would only have to underwrite the cost of walling it in and maintaining it. It's an insult to all the interested dog owners that we haven't acted on this very real need long before now."

"I apologize to the rest of the council on your behalf, Busby, for this waste of their time," Brewster said, playing to the audience.

What was with that guy? It was just a dog park. It probably wouldn't solve every dog owner in town's canine issues, but it would go a long way toward helping many. Solomon and Busby seemed to have found a viable solution.

"We wouldn't have to keep not discussing this issue if you'd just vote to put it on an agenda so we could deal with it once and for all," Busby replied.

Brewster opened his mouth to speak when another voice beat him to the punch. "Okay, gentlemen, this discussion has gone on long enough," the female voice said. Avery Wallace, the one woman on the council. "It's time we put this on our agenda to see where we all stand."

That said, it only took another minute for Busby to formally request the issue of the dog park go on the agenda. Porter McHugh immediately seconded. Wallace called the vote. Busby and McHugh voted yes. Brewster and Sheridan voted against it. Wallace voted for it.

"The vote is three for and two against. The ayes have it," she said.

"Madam Chair, I propose we discuss the proposal today rather than waiting until our next meeting as would normally be the case," Brewster said.

"Second!" Sheridan called.

Interesting tactic. Brewster must be counting on Busby and McHugh to be unprepared. Bad move, judging from what Solomon had told them about Busby's efforts to date.

Marianne expected Wallace to disapprove the idea, since the move would be a departure from council rules. But Wallace must have been ready to dispense with the topic, whichever way it went. "Councilmen Busby, McHugh and Sheridan? Are you willing to discuss the proposal today?"

Sheridan glanced first at Brewster and then gave his approval.

Busby and McHugh conferred privately for a minute and then said yes as well.

"How about that?" Wallace said. "We are all in agreement for once. Let that go on the record before we now discuss the specific proposal."

Wallace turned the floor over to Busby, who reached into a valise he'd set to the side of his chair and pulled out a file folder. He began by presenting the latest census data for the town and adding to it the numbers he'd collected in his semi-official survey. Approximately fifty-five percent of households were pet owners. Seventy percent of that group indicated an interest in having a dog park in town. He then distributed copies of a proposed budget for the project, then copies of two articles describing the ideal specifications for a dog park, then a diagram of a proposed layout based on those specifications, and finally a map and photo of the city property in question.

Brewster, Sheridan and Wallace took their time riffling through the documents or giving the appearance of studying them. The men were finished within two minutes. Wallace actually studied them. Busby and McHugh waited patiently.

"You've done your homework, Busby," Brewster said. "You've attempted to make a case for what a dog park should look like, but you fall short when it comes to the specific plot of land you've selected. True, it may not cost the city anything to purchase since we already own it, but there are other costs you haven't considered. And I'm not talking about the price of building and maintaining it. I'm interested in the intangible cost to the community, the noise created by excited, barking dogs that will constantly invade and interrupt the lives and well-being of those who do business in the same vicinity."

"Have you studied the map we distributed?" Busby asked. "There are no residences within a block and only one business, a funeral home whose clients are, well, dead people. Even if the dogs produced a low level of sound, and I'm not admitting that it would be produced, how would that 'invade and interrupt the lives and well-being' of those clients?"

Brewster's eyes shifted just slightly toward the audience. And only for a moment.

"I can speak to that, Madam Chair." A tall, dark-haired man dressed in a dark suit had risen in the audience."

"We're not taking comments from the audience yet," Wallace replied.

"But this topic directly concerns me and my business. I'm Gordon Kerimides. I own the funeral home that the proposed dog park would be next to. The Kerimides Funeral Home."

Wallace took a moment to consider Kerimides's statement before responding. "Okay. This topic has already traveled a somewhat out of the ordinary path. I'll allow you a moment to say your piece, as long as it is directly related to the topic of establishing a dog park at the designated location."

"Thank you," Kerimides said, offering a slight nod of his head. "In response to Councilman Busby's comment about my clients being dead people: Yes, I suppose it might appear that way to the uninformed. But our clients are also the loved ones of those dead people. Grieving loved ones whose lives have been torn apart by those deaths. Besides providing first-class preparation of the remains, we offer families and friends the peace and quiet they need to confront their loss and find the strength to move on." He paused, letting that thought sink in. "I shudder to think how that serenity will be shattered if it must compete with the piercing howling of a bunch of canines."

He actually let his voice waver on the word "shudder." Marianne couldn't help wondering if he occasionally delivered the eulogies in addition to his mortician duties. He certainly knew how to capture the attention of those assembled.

Everyone except Busby and McHugh.

"I think we can all agree that the loss of a loved one or friend can be devastating," Busby began, appearing to defer to Kerimides's argument. "In fact, Councilman McHugh and I recently attended the service of a mutual friend at your establishment. I was impressed with how the building had been designed to pay homage to the departed with the thick walls, deep carpeting, and long, high windows on the exterior wall of the two reception rooms. That particular day there was a tree-trimming crew just a hundred yards outside the building. This crew didn't just take down a few branches. They also chopped up what they'd cut while the service we were attending was underway."

He signaled to McHugh, who'd moved over to the audio-visual part of the room. McHugh stuck a flash drive in the computer and turned on the room's large screen. Marianne felt like she was a mourner sitting in a large room. "This is the interior of one of the Kerimides reception rooms," McHugh said. "The wife of the deceased gave us permission to film just before the service started. For only a minute. Just long enough to give you a feel for what someone attending a service here would see and hear. Mr. Kerimides nailed it when he spoke of the feeling of peace and quiet this place exudes."

At that point, the videographer took the viewer out of the room into the reception area on the other side of the door at the front of the building and turned the camera toward the front window. Outside, the tree-trimming crew could be seen busy at their task. "Do you hear anything outside?" McHugh asked the group. No one could deny there was no sound. At least that could be heard inside the building.

"So, to address Mr. Kerimides's concern, putting a dog park next to his building shouldn't interfere with the peace and quiet sought by the mourners at his services," Busby said. "So there," his tone seemed to say.

How fortuitous that the tree-trimming crew had shown up when they did to help Busby and McHugh make their point. Wait—that had been planned. Good thing they couldn't be heard inside the building. But then, Busby and McHugh wouldn't have shown the tape if it hadn't proved their point.

The room had gone quiet following their demonstration.

Brewster and Sheridan stared at their hands for several beats. Then Brewster spoke, his demeanor improving. "Interesting demonstration, gentlemen. But all you've proved is that a minor tree-trimming operation couldn't be heard from the reception area of the building. Not the actual rooms where services are held. You haven't shown us that a dog park wouldn't make more noise."

Busby screwed up his eyes as if trying to make sense of the statement. "Wouldn't that be a Catch-22 situation? To prove a dog park would make untenable noise for the funeral home would require it be a reality already, and that's the result we're discussing today." He raised his shoulders to supposedly punctuate his point.

"We don't disagree," Brewster answered. "But like you two, Councilman Sheridan and I also did some background work."

This time, Sheridan went to the AV equipment and inserted a flash drive.

The next thing heard was what sounded like a jet plane coming in for a landing, the volume so intense Marianne had to hold her hands over her ears.

The audio lasted only long enough to be irritating.

"That is the sound of the dog park in Shasta, our neighbor not too far from us, recorded last Saturday." Brewster addressed Busby directly. "That's what Mr. Kerimides as well as Councilman Sheridan and myself have been worried about. Who could possibly find peace and quiet when faced with that noise?"

Now Solomon was on his feet. "That was only audio, Brewster," he shouted. "How do we know it was recorded at a dog park?"

Busby joined him. "Even if it is the sound of a dog park, you could have assembled an army of dogs to make it sound worse."

Solomon wasn't finished. "We don't know it was actually a dog park. We didn't see where the sound was recorded."

"Don't insult us," Brewster replied. "We beat you at your own show."

While riding on the point he thought he'd made, Brewster moved the question, asking the council to immediately decide whether or not to approve the dog park.

"Not so fast, gentlemen," Wallace said. "I'm not convinced I know enough about this proposal to vote with any degree of certainty yet. I'm going to table this vote indefinitely until I'm satisfied I know enough."

"But Avery," Brewster cried.

"No, Tad. Not today. There's a lot at stake here. I don't want to make a precipitous decision."

When Wallace moved on to the few remaining items on the agenda, Marianne and Beau took their leave.

"A lot of fireworks back there," Beau said as they left the council chamber.

"I couldn't agree more. But why? Because it's a dog park or because there is opposition to the location?" she asked.

"That wasn't clear to me, either," Beau replied.

"I attended the council meeting more out of curiosity than to support either the proposal or Solomon. I hadn't expected to witness such deep acrimony on both sides. For a dog park? I got the sense there was more going on, but I couldn't figure out what."

He shot her a concerned look. "Please tell me you're not getting involved more than you already have. You have more than enough going on in your life at the moment."

"You're right, as usual. I'm glad you came with me to the meeting to keep me from getting too involved," she told him.

MARIANNE WAS in the kitchen the next day washing up the dinner dishes when her doorbell rang repeatedly. She met Beau coming from the den and they both nearly tripped over a barking Mortimer as they went to answer the door.

It was Solomon. At least she thought it was him. The man before them looked like he'd been left out in the rain.

"I need your help!" was the first thing out of his mouth.

"Come in, come in," Beau replied, pulling their visitor inside.

"Are you okay, Solomon?" Marianne couldn't help but ask.

"Do I look okay?" he screeched. "I'm the chief suspect in the murder of that funeral home owner."

Chapter Four

"Give us that again," Marianne said to Solomon once she and Beau had shown him into the house. "The funeral director, that guy who interrupted the council meeting, is dead?"

"Not just dead, murdered," Solomon replied. He continued to stand, even though Marianne indicated he should sit. But it wasn't easy, with Mortimer circling him and sniffing his pants for signs of Daisy.

"Sit down and tell us what you know," Beau said, picking up Mortimer. The dog stared back at Beau with an expression that seemed to say, "Are you sure he's okay?"

"Can't sit right now. Too fired up. But I'll tell you what I know."

Marianne and Beau did sit, leaving Solomon room to pace.

"I was just grilled by the sheriff and his deputy. Apparently Kerimides's sister-in-law, Stacia, found him this morning when she got to work. She works at the funeral home too. Found him in the display room, the area where the various caskets are shown. The sheriff wouldn't share any more details than that, apparently thinking if I was the killer, I might slip and reveal things only they know."

"How do they know he was murdered?" Marianne asked.

"He was strangled. They told me that much when I asked the same question."

"Why you?" Beau asked. "And why do you think you're the prime suspect and not just a person of interest they were interviewing to gain more background on the guy?"

Solomon pulled up behind an easy chair. "I, uh, just assumed that was the case. They asked where I was from ten last night to eight this morning, and I had to say I was at home until seven, when I had to take Daisy out. Only she could verify that. Did I jump too fast to the wrong conclusion?"

"Did you ask?" Marianne said. "They aren't obliged to tell you you're under suspicion unless they've got a solid case against you. Do they?"

"Not exactly. Well, no. I got so excited when the council decided to take up the proposal. That is, until Kerimides interrupted the proceedings. Things were going so well as far as approving the dog park. Until then, he was just a name Busby had shared with me. Not real. But once he spoke and then Brewster and Sheridan put on their performance, whatever hope I'd had for seeing this thing come to fruition died."

"We didn't get that impression," Beau said. "Avery Wallace slowed it down long enough to consider it further. Probably a wise move, if she really didn't know which side to come down on. It was pretty obvious to anyone who was there, she's in the catbird seat. Her vote decides it."

"Let's back up to the reason you think you were brought in for questioning," Marianne said. "Did they tell you why?"

Solomon rubbed the back of his neck. "The deputy who came to my door and asked me to accompany her to the sheriff's office didn't say much at all, simply that the sheriff would like me to come in to answer some questions about the proposed dog park. I had no idea how the sheriff had gotten involved with the dog park, but if there was anything I could do to show my support for the proposal, I wanted to do it."

"You didn't know about Kerimides until you got there?" Beau asked.

"No. Should they have told me?" Solomon asked hopefully.

"Not necessarily. They were testing you for your reaction. If you had killed the man, you might've been less cooperative. But since they didn't arrest you outright, they didn't have enough evidence. That works in your favor," Marianne said.

She was getting a strange vibe from Solomon's responses and actions. He wasn't telling them everything. Why? "Please sit down, Solomon. Beau and I need to get a firmer grasp on what you're telling us, and all that pacing isn't helping our brains."

"Oh, right. Sorry if whatever I've said thus far is a little mixed up. But that's how I feel right now."

"Understandable," she said. "But aside from being questioned, why do you think you're the prime suspect?"

Solomon rubbed his pants legs. Stalling?

"I, uh, went to see Kerimides the day after the council meeting."

Was he crazy? Kerimides was the last person Solomon should've been talking to. "Why? she asked.

He rolled his eyes. "In hindsight, it probably wasn't the smartest move I could have made, but at the time I thought maybe the two of us could come to some kind of agreement without involving the council."

"Did you get to talk to him?" Beau asked.

"Talk is too kind a term, but yeah, we did speak. After the council meeting when I heard that recording of the dog park in Shasta, I went online to check out the noise factor for myself. I'm embarrassed to say that was the first time I took that concern seriously. As it turns out, noise can be a deterrent to placing dog parks close to residences. But I also learned there are steps that can be taken to reduce the impact of noise. That prompted me to visit Kerimides to see if we couldn't find some kind of similar provision for our proposed dog park to make it a win-win situation. His response? Find another location for my dog park if I wanted to win."

"Did anyone else hear or see you when you were there?" Marianne asked.

"The woman in the office, I guess. I asked her where to find Kerimides, and she sent me to the display room. The place where families pick out their loved one's casket."

"Was that the sister-in-law?" Beau asked.

Solomon shrugged. "Maybe. I guess. She didn't introduce herself."

"Think carefully, Solomon," Marianne said. "Did you threaten him, either with words or physically, while you were there?"

"No! Wait. As I left, he called out something like, 'Your dog park is dead in the water.' I turned around and said, 'We'll just see about that.' But that wasn't meant as a threat. I couldn't just walk away without saying something."

Marianne exchanged an unobtrusive look with Beau. The sister-in-law most likely reported Solomon's visit to the sheriff's people, because they would have asked if Kerimides had any enemies. Did Solomon not realize the seriousness of his visit, or was he attempting to play it down? See how she and Beau reacted to it?

"Did any of the sheriff's people suggest you get an attorney before they questioned you?" Beau asked. (Their most recent class had been about the involvement of attorneys in the interrogation process.)

"No. Nor did I ask, since I thought I was just there to provide some information."

"Have you contacted one since?" Marianne asked.

Solomon shook his head. "No. I came here as soon as they took me back to my condo. Do you think I need one? I came to you guys because you told me you've been involved in solving some homicides in the past. I need your take on this whole situation."

"Our take?" Marianne's voice rose. She sought out Beau's reaction before proceeding. He nodded for her to go ahead. "The fact that they took you in to be questioned by the sheriff himself strongly suggests you not take your role lightly in this case. Had you not gone to speak with Kerimides, the spotlight might have missed you. The fact that you were seen by the woman in the office turns that spotlight up higher. Hopefully she didn't hear your parting comment. If she did, that could make matters even worse for you."

"I agree with Marianne," Beau said. "I'd think seriously about getting an attorney. At least have someone ready to step in if the sheriff involves you further."

"But I didn't kill him."

"Think like the sheriff," Marianne said. "Right now he's checking out all leads. You're on public record opposing

Kerimides from your comments at the council meeting. And you sought him out at his place of business and were seen there."

Solomon settled back in the chair and appeared to consider her points. "Okay, yeah, those are good points. But it's not like I had anything to gain from his death other than his opposition to the dog park would go away. The dog park would be a great help to me and Daisy as well as the other dog owners in town, but it's not a life-or-death issue with me."

"You wanted the unvarnished truth," she told him.

"I did. But now that you've put it to me like that, what do I do?"

"We already told you," Beau said, showing a tad bit of exasperation. "Get yourself a lawyer."

"It's not that I don't want to pay for one, but I'd prefer to wait until I've actually been charged with a crime to find somebody. What I really need is for the sheriff and company to find the real killer. At least find a more convincing suspect. How do I get them to do that? Or do I have to do the finding myself?"

Neither Marianne nor Beau responded to his last question. Was Beau thinking the same thing she was? She snuck a glance at her husband, who was gazing back at her with a raised eyebrow. After all these years of marriage, why was she having trouble reading his mind now? That raised eyebrow must mean he wasn't sure which way to go and was leaving it up to her. Right?

She bit the bullet. "No offense, but you aren't really trained to gather that type of information. But we know someone who is."

"That ex-cop friend of yours who you suggested before?" Solomon asked, as if challenging them.

"Yes, his is the first name that comes to mind," she replied. "Although there are others. And he is the ex-sheriff."

"Why not the two of you?"

"We're not at that point in our training yet," Beau said. Apparently he'd been okay with suggesting Rick but not them. They were in agreement.

"Would he even take the case?" Solomon asked.

"You'd have to ask," she replied. "He's still establishing his business."

"Thanks. I'll file away that suggestion."

What was with this guy? Why didn't he want to involve Rick? It was worth confronting him. "I don't get you, Solomon. You've been concerned enough to get a dog park in town that you went to a city council member. You even stood up in a council meeting and voiced your support for a dog park when it wasn't even time for public comment. Why are you so hesitant to call Rick Formero?"

Solomon licked his lips then rose and started to pace again.

"What's eating you, man?" Beau asked, apparently losing patience with their visitor.

Sighing, Solomon returned to his chair and flopped down. "I was new in town back when Formero was running for reelection. The wrong people convinced me to vote for the other guy, Jett Carmody. Not just vote—I helped campaign for him. I thought it was a way to get to know folks here in town. A few months later, after he'd been killed and the story about his links to illegal gambling came to light, I retreated from civic involvement."

"In other words, you're embarrassed to be seeking help from the very person you worked to defeat. Is that the deal?" Beau asked.

"You have a knack for cutting to the essence of a matter, Beau. Yeah, I guess that's my concern."

"Do you hear yourself?" Marianne asked. "You're unable to defend yourself against being charged with murder because once upon a time you made a bad decision and now you're afraid to face the consequences."

Solomon bent over and placed his hands around his head. Eventually, he removed his hands and lifted his head. "You make me sound like such a schmuck."

Neither Marianne nor Beau responded to his comment.

"Okay, guess I am a schmuck," Solomon finally said. "How do I get in touch with Rick Formero?"

Chapter Five

At six that evening, Marianne and Beau were summoned to Kat and Rick's house. "Did his text say why they wanted to see us?" Beau asked as they emerged from their car.

"We're the first to arrive if it's about the wedding plans," she replied. Perhaps it wasn't a meeting about those. Would Solomon have met with Rick already?

"Come in, come in," Kat said as she opened the door.

"We came as soon as we received Rick's text," Beau said. "What's up?"

"You know as much as I do," Kat said as she led them to the den, which was serving as Rick's temporary office until his new digs in one of the ranch's barns was ready.

"Thanks for coming so quickly," Rick said once they'd entered the den and were seated. He looked to his fiancée. "Would you please stay, too, Kat?"

She offered a perplexed look but also took a seat.

Rick remained standing. "I think you two know why you're here, but Kat doesn't. I met with a guy by the name of

Solomon Ridgedale a few hours ago. He said you two strongly suggested he get in touch with me."

"About that, Rick …" Beau began. "We decided not to contact you in advance and grease the skids for him because we didn't want to influence you one way or another whether to take his case."

"I figured that might be what happened."

Marianne cut to the chase. "Did you take his case?"

"I agreed to consider taking it, but I wanted to confer with the two of you first. Plus, since this might concern Katrina, I want her to sit in on this meeting also."

Marianne, Beau and Kat exchanged looks. This seemed so formal for Rick. Did he see a problem if he accepted Solomon's case?

Rick gave Kat a brief explanation of his visit with Solomon. "That's pretty much where things stand, right?" he asked Marianne and Beau.

"Pretty much," Beau said, "except how we got involved, which I'm guessing is why we're here."

"Partly," Rick replied. "I'll get to the rest shortly."

"Wait, before you go on, do I understand this is all about a dog park?" Kat asked.

"That's where it starts as well as how we got involved," Marianne told her. She told them how she'd first met Solomon through his dog and how that had led to their search for a dog park. "Beau and I attended a council meeting not long ago to observe for ourselves how the council felt about the dog park."

"It was an eye-opener," Beau added. "A dog park. Can you believe it? It sounded like such a good thing for the community, and from what Solomon had shared, it appeared that the two council members who supported the idea had done their homework to find the best place possible."

Marianne took over. "We had no idea how much antagonism the location for the proposed park had already aroused, particularly from this Kerimides guy, the one who owns, well, owned and ran the funeral home that would be adjacent to the proposed park. And then we learned from Solomon earlier today that Kerimides had been found dead this morning."

"And Solomon thinks he's the chief suspect because he spoke up at the council meeting and personally visited Kerimides to try to change his mind," Beau said. "That's where you come in, Rick. He wants you to find other persons of interest to take the onus off him as the supposed prime suspect."

"And that's it?" Rick asked.

"He wanted the two of us to investigate for him. We turned him down because we're busy with our course and because we don't have our credentials yet," Marianne responded. "We sent him your direction not just because we believe you'd be the perfect person to obtain the kind of information he wants but also because it involves a murder."

"We realized you'd have scruples about taking on an actual murder investigation which you'd feel should be handled by the sheriff," Beau put in, "but this wouldn't involve that type of investigation exactly. This would be information-gathering."

"Thanks for the background. He was rather guarded about why he was coming to me, other than to say the two of you had suggested me.

"I told him that before I agreed to sign on, I wanted to

speak personally with the sheriff to let him know what I might be doing. I don't want him to be caught off guard. Solomon wasn't crazy about my alerting the authorities to my involvement. Do the two of you have any idea why that might be?"

What was with Solomon? First, he didn't want to engage an attorney. And now he didn't want the sheriff to know he was privately looking into others' motives. "We can't answer that. We don't know him very well. So if you decide not to take his case, we'll understand," Marianne said.

Rick held up a hand. "Not so fast. Truth be told, I'm intrigued by this case, and I miss being directly involved in a homicide. I'll have to tread carefully if I take it on. Don't want Quinn to think I'm invading his territory."

"You don't have to get my permission to take on a case like this, Rick," Kat said. "I'll support whatever you decide."

"Thanks, hon. I figured you'd say something like that. I actually asked you to sit in because I think I may need your help as well as that of these two and probably your other partners in crime. Maybe we can get it accepted as extra credit for your course. How do you all feel about that?"

Marianne caught herself just as she was about to jump at Rick's proposal. It had been a while since they'd investigated a murder. Not since Jett Carmody got himself killed several months back. She made herself take a deep breath before responding. "I suppose that's something we could do." She caught Beau's eye. "Right, Beau?"

"Uh, sure, Rick. We'll do whatever we can, as long as our instructor approves?"

"I'll take care of that," Rick replied.

"We do need to remember we have a few other activities

underway," Kat said. "Like the remodel of the ranch. Getting you moved into your new office on the ranch. And, oh yes, a wedding."

"I can do this on my own, if that works better for all of you?" Rick said. "I just thought ..."

"That the rest of us would jump at the chance to investigate again? Or to use the proper terminology, help you gather information?" Marianne said. She looked from Beau to Kat. The two of them nodded their agreement.

"Okay, I'll visit Quinn at his home tonight. If he's on board, I'll gather the whole group tomorrow."

"Is this meeting a wedding update?" Syd asked as she selected a cookie from the plate Kat's housekeeper, Greta, had put out along with iced tea and coffee for the gathering about to happen.

"Tell me you're not postponing the wedding?" Micki was quick to ask. "I thought everything was coming together." She shot an accusing glance at Syd. "Unless the ranch house rehab is behind schedule?"

"Ladies, ladies," Trip Bonner pleaded. "Don't jump to conclusions. Let Kat explain."

"Thanks, Trip," Kat said, taking a seat herself. "Actually, it's Rick who's called this meeting. He'll join us in a minute. He had a last-minute call to make."

"Which I just ended," Rick said as he headed to where Kat was seated. "Thanks for coming on such short notice, everyone. I have accepted a case I wanted you all to know about. It's not a homicide per se, but it involves one. I could use some help with this one, even though you guys haven't completed your training yet."

"Wow, I thought we'd have to strong-arm you to ever be included in a case again," Micki said.

"Ever since I decided to open my own private investigations business, the plan has been for all of you to be part of it in some way. I just didn't plan for it to happen this soon."

"Don't keep us in suspense," Guy said. "Who got killed, and where do we come in?"

Rick looked to Marianne and Beau. "Okay if I take the lead on this?"

"Of course," Beau replied. "We just brought it to you."

"You guys know what this is about?" Syd asked, her tone accusing.

"I have a friend who thinks he's the prime suspect in a recent murder case. He came to Beau and me for help, and we sent him to Rick. Go ahead, Rick, this is your story now," Marianne said.

Rick took the floor, starting with the dog park and ending with Solomon being questioned by the sheriff. "After the references he gave me checked out and the quick look at his finances seemed okay, I visited privately with Brian Quinn to gain as much background on the case as he felt comfortable sharing and asked how strong a case they had against Solomon Ridgedale. As it turned out, Ridgedale is one of three or four other persons of interest they're considering, but Quinn was surprised the man had come away from what Quinn characterized as a routine interview thinking he was doomed.

"Now we're both wondering why that would be the case. Is the guy one of those people who always thinks he's guilty whether he is or not, or is he really guilty? Maybe I shouldn't have gone to Quinn in the first place because that may have raised Ridgedale higher on his list, but I couldn't accept this case without Quinn knowing I was taking it.

"I'm glad I felt I needed to inform Quinn that I'd pretty much decided to take the case, because his reaction was different than what I anticipated."

"Was he insulted that you thought his department couldn't handle it?" Kat asked.

"Just the opposite. Serendipity Springs is somewhat unique from other communities. Even though it doesn't define itself as a city, the founders felt a council form of government was important to home rule, even though they kept the mayor's job as a more ceremonial position. But they preferred to leave law enforcement to the county, which is why there's a sheriff's department as opposed to a police department. The sheriff reports to the county supervisors. The same group that appointed me special consultant to look into Carmody's murder.

"Anyway, with some if not all of the city council involved in this case, he thinks we, as an independent third party, might be in a better position to investigate, although he wants two of his deputies to sit in—Pilar Martinez and Colin Hastings, his best and most trusted deputies. I can attest to that. Other than Quinn, they were my best deputies."

"We couldn't ask for more," Guy said, apparently concerned about the legalities of this endeavor.

"Not so fast," Micki replied. "He's okay with our investigating this murder, but he doesn't trust us enough to do it on our own?"

"Micki, we can't kid ourselves that we ever investigated

those other murders on our own," Kat told her. "Rick was always there in the background. And not just through me. You all checked in with him at different times."

Rick gave his fiancée a side hug. "Thanks, Kat. Let me clarify," he said to the others. "The deputies won't be acting as lead investigators. They'll simply be there to grease the skids for you and give our interviews credibility by adding an air of official authority."

The others exchanged looks but didn't respond.

"Quinn's got a good head on him," Rick added. "Plus, he was trained by the best." He smiled.

"I'm in," Syd said. "How about the rest of you?"

When everyone but Micki nodded their assent, all seven of them turned their eyes on her. "Oh, okay," she responded, putting her hands up, surrender-style.

"Now that we've settled that, what's our goal?" Syd asked. "To prove Ridgedale isn't guilty or to find the real guilty party, if that's the case?"

"Neither. The best we can hope to do is find others with as much motive, opportunity and means to kill the funeral home owner as Ridgedale."

"But you don't know for sure if this guy is innocent?" Micki asked.

"He could be guilty. My agreement with him is if I find absolute proof of his guilt, I'm out. But whatever I've discovered up to that point he can turn over to his attorney in his defense."

"But he hasn't engaged an attorney yet?" Guy, their very own attorney, asked.

"No. He says he will if and when he's charged."

Guy narrowed his eyes. "Do you buy that?"

"No, not really. He says he had some bad experience with one in the past and therefore avoids them as much as possible. I told him I didn't completely buy that explanation and I expected the absolute truth from him about anything else I might uncover if I took his case."

"Sounds suspicious to me," Guy said.

"Good!" Rick said. "That's one of the reasons I wanted you included in this group even though you're not in the PI intern class. If you sign on, I'd like you to look into his reason for avoiding legal representation as long as possible."

"Thanks for the confidence in me," Guy replied. "Give me a minute to think about it. I want to hear the rest of the details about this case before I decide."

"Fair enough," Rick said. "Yeah, as for those details, let me tell you what I've learned so far. The victim was Gordon Kerimides, a forty-five-year-old funeral home owner. He and his late brother were co-owners until his brother disappeared in a boating accident a few years back. His body was never found, but he was presumed dead. Kerimides's body was found draped over an open casket in the display room of his business. He'd been strangled by what was probably a thin wire, a dog collar around his neck, although it's thought that was just for show. None of those details are being released to anyone else, especially the media."

"Ooh, that's horrible," Micki said. "His killer couldn't just shoot, knife or poison him?"

"Good point," Rick said. "Whoever did it staged it for a purpose. That's another point I need one of you to look at. Marianne, you're the playwright, but since you thought of it, Micki, have at it."

"Who else does the sheriff suspect?" Beau asked.

"That's where you all come in. So far they've only zeroed in on Councilman Busby, maybe Councilman McHugh because Kerimides was opposing their proposal for a dog park. There's also the sister-in-law, who discovered the body. She apparently still questions the disappearance of her late husband."

"What about the other council members?" Marianne asked. "Although it would appear they were Kerimides's allies, maybe there was some kind of falling out since the meeting we observed."

"Seems like we've moved from my getting your buy-in to actually planning this project," Rick said. "Do I hear any nays?"

No one said anything.

"Okay, then, let's try this out. This is a new way of us working together as a team with my leadership. We'll figure this out as we go. If problems pop up, let's discuss them. One more thing. Since the business isn't completely operational and you're not qualified interns yet, we're doing this gratis, other than expenses. That work for everyone?"

His team of seven—Marianne and Beau, Syd and Trip, Micki and Guy and Kat—all nodded.

Kat pulled out her laptop. "You've already made a few assignments, Rick. I'll start a list so we'll all have a record."

"You don't mind being our secretary?" Syd asked.

Kat chuckled. "This isn't a women's rights thing, Syd. I'm his partner. I know his mind better than any of you, so I'm in a better position to summarize his thoughts."

Syd nodded. "I get you."

"Thanks, Kat," Rick said. "Excuse me, all. I'll be right back." He returned a minute later pulling a large white board on rollers. "I seem to think best when I'm laying out my plans on one of these."

They spent the next hour identifying who would do what.

"Are you sure we won't get into any trouble helping you investigate?" Marianne asked. "We're so close to completing our course, I don't want to hurt our chances of seeing it through."

"Good point. I forgot to add 'clear your participation with your coach.' I'll do that tomorrow. Maybe we can even get your work on this case added as extra credit," Rick said.

After they broke up, Micki stood in front of the white board, her head cocked.

"What are you thinking, Mick?" Kat asked her. "Did we miss something?"

"Not as far as this Kerimides murder is concerned," Micki answered. "I'm just impressed with how quickly Rick and the rest of us put this plan together. Everyone participated, and no one appeared to be opposed. I think we should try something like this as we proceed with your wedding plans. I don't suppose you have a second white board?"

Chapter Six

*D*eputy Pilar Martinez met them at their favorite coffee shop half an hour before their appointment with Kerimides's sister-in-law, but she turned down anything except a glass of iced tea. "I've been trying to avoid the carbs ever since my darling Bernardo arrived on the scene."

She must be succeeding. Around five four, her dark hair pulled back in a ponytail, the new mother appeared to have shed every pound of baby weight and maybe even a few more.

"Thanks for meeting us before we interview Stacia Kerimides," Beau said. "We wanted to thank you in advance for helping us."

The deputy eyed them with something between a smile and a scowl. "That's not necessary."

"Because it was an order?" Marianne guessed.

Pilar studied her hands. "Uh, yes."

"None of us is totally happy with this arrangement. But Beau and I understand why Rick and your boss, the sheriff, want things this way," Marianne said.

"Marianne and I are prepared to move ahead with it," Beau said. "We hope you are, too."

The deputy didn't respond immediately. "Okay, I'm willing to give it a try. Just so we agree, I'm in charge. I'll turn the interview over to you two after I've set things up."

"Agreed," Beau said, checking Marianne, who nodded.

Pilar rose. "I'll meet you on the steps of the funeral home's entrance."

Ten minutes later, the threesome walked together to Stacia Kerimides's office.

"Thank you for seeing us," Deputy Martinez said to the woman as the sister-in-law greeted them at her door. "This is Marianne and Beau Putnam. They are helping the sheriff's department with the investigation of your brother-in-law's murder. We realize it's early days after what happened to him and you must still be in shock, but this is the best time for us to gather information."

Stacia Kerimides pulled a tissue from somewhere and dabbed at her eyes before answering. "Okay," she replied tentatively. "As long as you understand I'm still working my way through this situation."

Marianne judged the woman to be between forty and fifty, around five seven. Her dark eyes—deep brown—were set too close to her nose, a nose too short for her long face. Her auburn hair fell about four inches below her collar. Still, she was attractive in her own way.

Pilar nodded at Marianne, turning the interview over to her. "First, my husband and I offer our sympathies."

"Thank you. What you'll probably learn from others—so I might as well be up front with you—I wasn't the biggest fan of my brother-in-law. He would have gotten rid of me a long time ago except I have iron-clad partnership and personal services contracts, signed when my husband was still alive and an active partner in this business. I realize that might put me at the top of your list of suspects, but I didn't kill him. I just had the monumental bad luck to find his body."

Momentarily thrown by this admission, Marianne shifted gears with her first question. She searched her brain for the best way to grab hold of this nugget of information and milk it for all it was worth. They'd been studying effective interrogation methods in class. She hadn't realized she'd be challenged with this golden opportunity to try them out so soon. "Why didn't you and your brother-in-law get along?"

Stacia flipped a strand of hair. "Tom, my presumed-dead husband from a boating accident several years ago, only agreed to become Gordon's partner if I was also included in the deal. Gordon went along with it as long as I only performed undertaking duties as a backup. That's how I wound up handling most of the administrative part of the business and officiating some services where there is no religious representative."

"Tell us about your brother-in-law. You were probably closer to him than anyone," Marianne told the woman.

Stacia considered her response for a few beats. "Gordon was a very private person. He didn't have many friends. Tom was probably closest to him. After Tom's disappearance, Gordon retreated even further into himself. Being a mortician was a good job fit."

"How about friends?" Beau asked.

"He didn't have much of a social life, at least as far as I'm aware. Over the years he may have had a few men friends, but not like they were buddies or anything. Nor was Gordon the type to join bowling teams or the like. He never had a girlfriend that I'm aware."

She had described the picture of a very lonely man. At least a very private one. How did that mesh with his strong objection to the dog park due to the anticipated noise?

"Let's go back to how the two of you ran the business," Beau said. "What did you mean when you said you did most of the administrative part?"

"All three of us dealt with the money end while Tom was around. After his disappearance, Gordon took it over, saying it was one way he could help me through my grief. I very stupidly let him do it. I still bill our clients and pay the bills, but he handles the investment end. He took over almost all the undertaking duties. When he needed to be away or was too sick to work, which was rare, we brought in a substitute.

"Although I ordered everything having to do with the services, Gordon ordered anything related to the undertaking part."

"Help me understand what's so important about under-taking," Marianne said. The profession had never appealed that much to her.

"Have you lost anyone close to you lately?"

Marianne and Beau exchanged looks. "Acquaintances, perhaps?" Marianne replied.

Deputy Martinez shook her head.

"Before I answered your question, I wanted to be sure I wasn't stepping on the memory of any recent losses," Stacia said. "We have a double commitment here. Of course, we want to help the mourners find closure in their grief. But our first commitment is to provide the deceased with our best professional care of their remains. Thus, the mortician is the star, as bizarre as it may seem. Gordon wanted that role. No sharing of the spotlight."

"What happens now?" Beau asked. "Will you take over his tasks?"

She sat forward and folded her hands. "I haven't decided yet. Obviously, it wasn't appropriate for me to deal with his remains. Our sub is doing that, and he's also agreed to stay on until I do decide."

"Let's talk about your discovering him," Marianne said. "You've done this already for the first officers on site, but we'd like to hear your story again in your own words."

Stacia released a breath. "I usually went out of my way to avoid him, but that morning I needed his signature on the contract to renew our landscaping services. It was due the next day, and he'd been putting it off while he was fighting this dog park. He wasn't answering my calls, so I wandered down to the embalming area. I rarely went there because he made it clear I wasn't welcome there. The place was a mess, but he wasn't there. That wasn't like Gordon. He was a neatness freak. He wouldn't have left the area looking like that. Plus, he would have locked it up." She turned to Deputy Martinez. "Your people took numerous photos of the area, in case Mr. and Mrs. Putnam need to get a better feel for what I found." She switched her attention to Marianne and Beau. "Or I can take you there when we're done talking here?"

Marianne resisted the urge to shudder. The photos would provide her with enough setting of the scene. "Thank you. I can't speak for my husband, but that won't be necessary for me right now."

"I'll pass, too," Beau said. "Especially since the victim was found elsewhere, right?"

"Yes," Stacia replied. "Obviously, something happened in the embalming area, but I found Gordon's body in the display room. You have pictures of that also."

"I would like to see that room for myself," Marianne said. "And that was around eight ten?"

"Five after eight, to be exact," Stacia replied.

"Was anyone else in the building at that time?" Beau asked.

"Our custodian, Billy Sampson, but he was still having coffee in the break room. The funeral director, Warren Meek, doesn't come in until eight thirty. Billy heard my screams and came running immediately."

"How soon did he join you?" Beau asked.

Stacia raised her brows. "In about a minute or two. Does that matter?"

"Just getting a better feel for the scene," he replied.

"He's somewhere in the building, if you'd like to talk with him as well as me?" she asked.

"Maybe later," Marianne told her. "Before we do that, are you aware of anyone who would want to kill your brother-in-law?"

Stacia's eyebrows moved closer together. "I can think of a few people who didn't like him, but I don't see them killing him."

Beau seized upon her comment. "Who didn't like him?"

"I'm sure you're aware of his dispute with a few of the city council members? Drake Busby and Porter McHugh, to be specific. Over a silly dog park. If you haven't already, I would start with the two council members."

"Did he discuss his concerns about the dog park with you?" Beau asked.

"No. I only heard about his speaking to the council from Warren Meek afterwards. It was so unlike Gordon. He never got involved in civic matters."

"Supposedly he was concerned how the noise from the dog park would affect your mourners," Marianne said. "Do you agree?"

"Gordon rarely paid heed to the needs of our mourners," Stacia replied. "Only if they had a concern about how the remains were handled. I suspect something more was involved with the dog park."

Marianne shot a quick look at Beau. "Something more? What do you mean?" she asked.

Stacia shrugged. "I have no idea. Like I said, Gordon rarely spoke with me, especially about this dog park. He never owned a dog, but I doubt that was behind his opposition. I'd look more closely at the proposed location for the park, in that open field just behind our building. I wouldn't put it past Gordon to have had his sights on it for future expansion of our business. Not that he ever discussed that possibility with me."

"Can you think of any others who didn't care for him?" Marianne pushed, since the council members were already on their list. Though they apparently didn't get along with each other, this woman probably saw more of the victim than anyone else. "Disgruntled customers, other relatives, friends?"

"Other than Tom, Gordon had no other relatives. I

already mentioned his lack of friends. By *customers* I assume you mean the loved ones of our actual customers? Yes, every business has those who don't agree with the way their situation has been handled, even funeral homes. Especially funeral homes, because our business concerns emotions. But I wouldn't characterize them as disgruntled. Occasionally, someone isn't happy with how the body was prepared. Gordon took care of those. Rarely did he update me on the outcome, but since we haven't been sued, I'd have to say he was successful."

Marianne signaled to Deputy Martinez that she was ready to terminate the interview and rose. The other three came to their feet in response.

"Unless it's absolutely necessary, I'd prefer you view the display room on your own. It's still difficult for me to go in there," Stacia said.

Although Marianne had hoped to read the woman's reaction to the room, she didn't push. She didn't know just what she was hoping to find when she saw the room for herself, but perhaps she could get a better read if she wasn't assessing Stacia's body language at the same time.

The yellow police tape still cordoned off the display room, although at first glance nothing appeared out of place. Six different types of caskets took up most of the space, although they weren't crowded together. Four were set up on tables and two were on the floor. Each was strategically placed off by itself. Was that so loved ones making a selection wouldn't feel claustrophobic, or was the room just that large?

Deputy Martinez led the way to one of the caskets sitting on the floor. "This is where she found Kerimides's body."

The casket was a dark wood. Inside, it was lined with

peach satin. A tiny peach satin pillow rested on one end. "This is it?" Beau asked, tilting his head. "They haven't cleaned it up or brought in a replacement?"

The deputy shook her head. "No, this is the very one. There wasn't much to clean up. No blood, anyway. Sorry, I hope my mention of blood didn't gross you out?"

"Not to worry," Marianne reassured her. "We've seen worse."

"Some body oil did get on the outside, but that has been cleaned up. You've got the photos of the body, but would you like me to demonstrate the actual position?"

"Yes, please do," Beau replied. "We don't want to come off as ghoulish, but the more we know about this crime scene, the better idea we'll have about how it happened. Well, you know?" He must have added that last part when he realized he might have insulted her professional knowledge.

Martinez handed them her jacket and the small valise she carried. Then she draped her back over the side of the casket. "Of course, he was five inches taller than me, so as you can see from the photos, his head was a little further inside this thing. With a three-fourths-inch-wide dog collar around his neck."

"Yes, the dog collar. Have you ever come across one used as a means of murder?" Marianne asked.

Martinez pulled out of her position as victim. "No, but you are aware that he was strangled with something else first and the dog collar was used as adornment, right?"

"Oh, right. Has the actual means of strangulation been determined yet?" Marianne asked, kicking herself mentally. She knew the dog collar had only been used to make a point.

"The forensics analysis of crime scenes takes longer than

other aspects of the investigation. This slows us down in some ways, so we learn to put a pin in some assumptions until we have all the scientific evidence. But in this case, given the bruising on his neck, we're fairly certain he was choked with a thin wire of some sort."

Marianne took a few steps back from the casket and attempted to visualize how the murder took place. It didn't take much imagination to understand why the man had met his end, but the way it happened was taking more brain power. How had he been overpowered enough for someone to slip a wire around his neck? "He wasn't killed here, was he?" she asked Martinez.

The deputy's eyes narrowed. "I wasn't hiding that part from you. We, the sheriff and I, wanted to see if you figured it out for yourself."

"The embalming room!" Beau cried, catching on. "Which explains the mess you found there."

"You've seen photos of the guy before his death. It would have taken a lot to take him out, which probably explains the contusion on the back of his head. The medical examiner says it was delivered pre-death. In other words, it wasn't the result of somehow hitting his head against the casket after strangulation. The disarray of the embalming room probably occurred as part of that struggle."

"Probably?" Marianne asked.

"We can't be sure until someone who knows their way around an embalming room can review the current state of the room's contents. Mrs. Kerimides is too close to the scene to do that. The guy they've used on occasion as a backup has been available, but the state forensic tech has been out of town until tomorrow. He's the only one the state has with knowledge of the various chemicals and other elements used in the embalming process."

"Why are we interviewing Stacia Kerimides now if we don't have answers to that situation?" Marianne asked.

Martinez took her time reclaiming her jacket and valise. "For now, the sheriff wants to keep her part in this case separate. We think you can develop a clearer perspective on her role in the murder if you just focus on her and not the murder scene."

Beau shot a glance at Marianne, a question in his eyes. This was news to both of them. Had Quinn decided he could use their services to size up the sister-in-law but not discover the murderer? Or was Martinez attempting to shut them out? It would be understandable if the woman resented outsiders being brought in to do her job.

For now, Marianne would accept this scenario. Beau would go along with her. "Oh. All right. That being the case, if Beau agrees, I think we're done with her for now. But we'd like to talk to the custodian and funeral director as soon as that can be arranged."

"Uh, okay." Beau turned to the deputy. "Thanks for sitting in with us today. We'll contact you if we need more information from the lady."

Bless his heart. He was putting their best spin on being shut out of a key part of the investigation. She could do the same. "Please thank Mrs. Kerimides for her time. And thank you as well."

"What was all that about?" Beau asked once they were in the car, having left Martinez behind with Stacia Kerimides.

Marianne rubbed her neck. "If I didn't know better, I'd say we received the brush-off. Polite but firm. Rather than make a scene, I thought we should give the appearance of acceding to the company line. At least until we've conferred with Rick and Kat. But don't for a minute think I'm ready to leave our efforts at that. That embalming room holds the key to the murder, and I intend to find out what that is."

Chapter Seven

"We're almost at Councilman Busby's florist shop," Kat said to Micki from behind the wheel, "and you haven't said a thing since I picked you up. Where is the real Micki Demetrius?"

Micki, who'd been looking out the side window, shifted position and offered Kat an apologetic smile. "She's here. She's just analyzing our situation."

Kat shot a quick glance at her passenger. "Marianne and I do the analyzing in this group. You come up with the brilliant ideas, which I'd be delighted to hear any time before we get there, since I've never interviewed a councilperson before."

"A councilperson supposedly pro dog park. That part I get. But that puts both Busby and his cohort, Councilman McHugh, high on the list of suspects. Our interviewing skills will be put to the test."

"Since when have you ever backed away from a challenge?" Kat asked.

Micki snorted. "I have to admit, my journalistic curiosity has been piqued. But you know me, once I get started, it's not always easy for me to stop pressing. What am I supposed to do if that occurs with these two distinguished representatives of the city?"

Kat reached across the seat and touched Micki's forearm. "Maybe that's why Rick paired me up with you. I'm supposedly the peacemaker of the group. But have no fear. In this instance, I say go for it. They're used to being questioned in council meetings."

Busby's Blooms was located on the edge of downtown Serendipity Springs. Micki suddenly stopped in her tracks as they left the car. "Ooh, a chill just ran down my back," she told Kat. "I've avoided flower shops ever since we tracked down the killer of Olivia Schwimmer's husband. Don't you remember? Syd took it upon herself to confront the culprit when we weren't available soon enough for her and got herself locked in the cooler for her impatience."

"You're right! I'd forgotten. Not to worry. We're supposed to meet Deputy Colin Hastings before we go in, since Sheriff Quinn has required his staff to sit in on our interviews. He'll keep us out of harm's way."

Rick had assured them that Hastings had been one of the good guys who'd worked for him while Rick was still in office the year before and struggling with deteriorating staff relations. Hastings had stayed on when Quinn was named sheriff.

Deputy Colin Hastings waited for them outside. Tall and dark-haired, he reminded Kat of a soap opera star. "Good morning, ladies," he said, blocking their way. "Do we need to confer about our roles before going in?"

"We're clear. You're here representing the sheriff to give our interview an air of authority," Micki replied.

"Just so you know, I'm going along with this setup

because the boss asked me to and because I already know and trust you, Ms. Faulkner. But I don't feel comfortable with the arrangement. If this guy is our killer, you two may be putting yourselves in more danger than you bargained for."

"We appreciate your concern, Colin," Kat said. "But Rick, my fiancé and the former sheriff, has every confidence in you to not only protect us but also facilitate our meeting with Councilman Busby."

The firm set of Hastings's jaw softened a little. "I'm willing to give this a shot, but if anything gets out of kilter, any future dealings with persons of interest will have to be reconsidered."

"Fair enough," Micki said. "The same goes for us if you don't give us the support we need."

Kat resisted the urge to roll her eyes at Micki's comment. Had they blown their partnership with the law already? She could understand Hastings's reluctance to work with them, two senior women, but they knew what they were doing. They'd done this kind of thing more than once, and now, thanks to their PI course, they were even better prepared how to handle themselves. "Don't take that as a challenge, Deputy. Just be aware that your boss trusts us enough to let us talk with Councilman Busby. Once we've met with the man, we hope you'll feel the same way."

Now that Micki had planted the idea in her brain, Kat tried not to cringe as they walked past the cooler on their way to Busby's office. She focused instead on the beautiful spring blooms and potent floral fragrances along the way. Their heady fragrance was hard to ignore.

Busby looked up from his laptop when they entered. "I've

been expecting someone from the sheriff's office," he said, "although not three of you."

Hastings explained why Kat and Micki were with him.

"Should I be concerned or pleased?"

"You should be concerned only if you killed Gordon Kerimides," Colin answered.

"I did no such thing!" Busby said, rising.

"Then you shouldn't have anything to worry about," Micki said, taking center stage. "Besides, your friend Solomon Ridgedale told our friends Marianne and Beau Putnam to give you the benefit of the doubt."

"You know Ridgedale?" he asked.

"Tangentially," Kat replied.

Busby returned to his seat. "Well, then. Let's get on with the inquisition, er, interview. What do you need to know?"

"Let's start with your whereabouts two nights ago," Kat said.

"I was here until ten that night putting together a table piece for a customer's dinner party the next night. After that, I went home and was there the rest of the time until eight the next morning."

"Can anyone verify that?" Micki asked.

He sat back. "No. I was alone. But you can check with my client to confirm I delivered the flowers at nine that morning."

"In other words, you could have slipped into the funeral home and murdered Gordon Kerimides at any time during that night," Kat said.

"But I didn't," he pleaded.

"You've gone on record vowing to make him sorry for his stand against the dog park," Kat said.

"Yes, that's true. But that certainly wasn't a death threat. And I wasn't the only one he'd crossed. Have you talked to Councilman McHugh yet? Like me, he wasn't happy with Kerimides's role in the dog park issue."

"Did you ever meet Gordon Kerimides?" Kat continued, skirting a response to his question.

Busby pushed away from his desk and ran a hand along the back of his neck. "I've known Gordy since high school. We both lived in Shasta. Serendipity Springs was in its infancy then. We even toured Europe together in a boy band the summer after our graduation. We returned to the States to go our separate ways the next several years until we both opened our own businesses here. Since then, I've had little to no contact with him other than flower delivery to services at the funeral home."

"What about recently? Did you run into him then?" Micki asked.

"Not exactly. Well, sorta. Porter McHugh and I took it upon ourselves to sit in on a funeral, with the permission of the widow of the deceased. We wanted to hear the supposed outside noise for ourselves."

"Was that when the video that was introduced at the council meeting was taken?" Micki asked.

He swallowed. "Yes, although we'd already done some reconnaissance the day before when we wandered around the place on our own. That's when we got the idea to record the noise level from the outside that could be heard during an actual funeral. We managed to walk in with no one the wiser. Spent several minutes in the chapel and didn't hear a thing. As we emerged into the reception area, we ran smack into Kerimides. From the look in his eyes, I could tell he recognized me from our teen years, although he didn't mention it."

"Did you talk to him?" Micki asked.

"He stopped us and asked if we were lost. Porter answered for us. Told him we were there to check out the dimensions of the chapel for a client. That didn't satisfy Kerimides. He asked for the client's name. That's when Porter turned it over to me, having given me a few seconds to work on our story. I told him we were developing a preplanned funeral proposal for a client we weren't at liberty to name."

"Did he believe you?"

"If only. He called us by name and demanded to know why we were really there. Porter gave him half the story. Told him we were checking out the noise level in the chapel. He left out the part about videotaping the next day during a service. But just that much was enough to incense Kerimides. He said he'd be reporting us to the city council chair, Avery Wallace, and letting the local media know we were not only trespassing but also attempting to disparage his business."

"Did he follow through on those threats?" Kat asked.

"He must have called Avery, because she contacted Porter and me separately two days later. She couldn't really do much other than ask us to stay away from Kerimides. She doesn't like to rock the boat and put the council in a bad light. By that time, we'd already been to the funeral, unbeknownst to Kerimides, but like I said, with the widow's permission. Neither of us told her that part."

"What about the local media?" Micki asked.

"If he did contact them, he didn't find anyone to support him, because I saw nothing online."

"You realize that your position on the dog park—directly

in opposition to the victim—puts you high on the list of suspects," Marianne said.

"That's just circumstantial. There are a lot of issues that come before the council that others don't agree with. That doesn't mean I'd kill them."

"Okay," Micki said evenly. "Who else might want to kill the man?"

"I have no idea. Like I said before, I haven't had much to do with him in recent years. Even in our teen years, he was a strange bird. We never were really close friends. You want to know more about who he was these days, check with Brewster or Sheridan, since they've carried his water about the dog park. Ask yourselves why."

"Do you own a dog, Councilman?" Kat asked, switching topics.

Busby stared at her like he hadn't heard the question. "No. Why do you ask?"

"I just wondered if that was your reason for supporting the dog park."

"No, it wasn't," he answered.

"Then why did you support it?" Micki asked.

"Why shouldn't I? It was something the community needs."

"Was it your idea?" Micki pursued when he didn't elaborate.

"No."

They had to do better asking open-ended questions. "Tell us about the circumstances that brought the idea of a dog park to your attention," Kat said, hoping they'd garner more information than had been forthcoming so far.

"Is that really necessary?" Busby asked.

"We won't know until you tell us," Kat said.

"It's personal. Even though I'm a public figure, my private life should remain private."

"If your private life affects this case, we need to know about it," Hastings said.

The room went silent while the three of them stared at a defiant Busby. He was the first to cave. "Okay, okay. I have to trust you to keep this to yourselves. There's this woman I'm interested in. She owns this mammoth dog. If I have any hope of getting close to her, I have to accept this creature as well. I was drinking with Solomon Ridgedale one night when he brought up the subject of a dog park. He described how difficult it was keeping his own dog from tearing apart his condo because it didn't have a place to expend all its energy. Since his problem sounded a lot like mine, I agreed to help him get it passed by the city council."

Kat and Micki exchanged looks. Though Busby was acting like he was revealing some big secret thanks to their pressure, Kat wasn't convinced. If anything, it was a charming story, not something to keep under wraps. Was Micki having the same doubts?

"We're all in favor of romance, Councilman, but why is your interest in this woman so private? Is she married?" Kat asked.

"Is she unaware how you feel?" Micki added.

"Neither," Busby replied. "My divorce was final two years ago. She's a widow. We're just both ... private people."

"Really?" Micki's tone was skeptical. "When you ran for a seat on the council, you gave up your private life." She considered her own words. "Good story. It probably is true, but that's not what's behind your support of a dog park."

"In fact, you weren't always a supporter, were you? Never mind, I already know," Kat said. "I've been going through past council minutes. Solomon Ridgedale has been trying to get on the agenda long before you thought the dog park was a good idea. Something happened to gain your interest. I'm guessing it was when Ridgedale discovered the property the city already owned could be the location of the park. The property next to the Kerimides Funeral Home."

"No. That was just a coincidence, although it made his proposal stronger," Busby said.

"What did change your mind?" Kat asked.

"Ridgedale had been trying to collar me and the other council members for some time with his dog park proposal. It really didn't click with me until a canine came into my life."

Busby shot up. "I hope you're finished, because I need to get out on the floor." He waited for them to leave and then followed right behind them.

Outside, Deputy Hastings was ready to put a period on the interview. "Okay, you've talked to the councilman. I'll let Sheriff Quinn know this one can be checked off."

Micki held up her hand, her fingernails boasting a fresh new coat of bright red. "Not so fast, Hastings. It usually takes us at least two interviews before we either eliminate a person of interest or decide they're a likely suspect. We have a little more homework to do on Councilman Busby before we're ready to put him in either category."

"Ladies, I'm booked for the next several hours," he replied, his tone polite but firm. "I need to move on."

"That works for us," Kat said. "Micki and I need time to pick through his comments and decide where we go next.

We're scheduled with you again this afternoon with Avery Wallace." She didn't leave room for debate.

Hastings grimaced like he was about to get a flu shot. "Okay. I'll see you then."

"We've got our work cut out for us, Mick," Kat told her friend once they were back in her car.

"Yeah, we need to unearth more background on Drake Busby," Micki replied.

"Not just that. We need to convince Deputy Hastings we're not just two old biddies who have the ear of the sheriff."

Chapter Eight

Deputy Pilar Martinez wasn't available to accompany Syd and Trip until late morning, so Syd took the opportunity to show her husband around the results of her remodeling efforts at Kat's ranch house. "I wanted you to be the first to see my progress, since you're the one who helped me past the wall I'd hit to find the inspiration I needed to move on."

Trip stood stock still inside the door, taking in the great room. With Kat's permission, Syd had removed all traces of the elegant English drawing room the previous owner had installed and replaced them with the vibrant colors of the Southwest. "It's stunning, Syd. You've brought Arizona to Florida."

"Oh. Do you think that's how she'll see it?"

"Isn't that what you intended?" he asked.

"I suppose it might look that way, but no. You reminded me of the Native American blanket that gave me comfort while I was recovering from breaking my ankle after I fell off my horse. That was the feeling I wanted to bring to this room."

"But weren't we at a dude ranch in Arizona at the time?"

Why did he have to be so factual at times? "True ..."

"How did you describe what you had in mind when you got Kat's buy-in?"

She tried to recall that meeting. It had taken place months ago, about the same time Kat and Rick got engaged and Rick was on the verge of starting his own PI business. The whole business blended together at the moment. "I don't remember telling her how the blanket had inspired me, but I did compare my concept to a generalized Native American blanket and handed her a palette filled with the main colors I had in mind."

"Then this won't come as a surprise," he said. "What are you worried about?"

Something definitely was bothering her about the results of her decorating efforts now that she examined them through Trip's eyes. "The colors are gorgeous, aren't they?" Then it came to her. "But they don't reflect a wedding very well, do they?"

Trip took a few steps into the room and gazed about him. "Well, there's definitely no white or pastels here. But are those what Kat wants?"

"I need to get with Micki. She appointed herself wardrobe and décor manager for the event."

Trip checked his watch. "That'll have to wait until later. It's about time for us to meet with Deputy Martinez."

The offices for Dr. Porter McHugh, DDS as well as councilman, were part of a larger office building located in the eastern edge of town. Deputy Martinez got out of her car at the same time Syd and Trip pulled into the parking lot. "The sheriff asked me to meet with you before the three of us talk to Dr. McHugh just so we're all on the same page regarding these interviews."

"Right," Trip replied. "Rick Formero told us that was part of the deal he made with Sheriff Quinn in order for us to investigate the murder."

"Yes. Since it's somewhat unusual, well, unprecedented for Sheriff Quinn, it's important that everyone involved be aware of the ground rules and agree to follow them." She spent the next few minutes going over said ground rules, mainly that she'd do the introductions and that she'd be in charge of the rest of the interview. They could ask questions, but she'd stop them at any time such questions strayed beyond anything related to the case. "Are we clear?" she asked both individually.

Trip said yes. Syd attempted to be diplomatic. "We realize you've been placed in unusual circumstances and appreciate your willingness to work with us. So, yes, Trip and I understand the conditions of our involvement."

Dr. Porter McHugh had set aside a half hour in his otherwise full schedule to speak with them. "Before you start," he said, once they were ensconced in his private office, "I want to go on record saying I'd only met the guy, Kerimides, once. That was when Busby convinced me to go with him to check out the noise levels from the outside in the funeral home. I didn't kill the man."

At that point, Deputy Martinez, her explanation of their presence having been cut off already by McHugh's statement, now went into the part about who Syd and Trip were and why they were there.

McHugh, the top of whose desk held nothing, opened a

top drawer and pulled out a paper clip, which he began unbending. "Rather unusual, isn't it?"

"Actually, consultants to the police are being used more frequently," Martinez replied. Syd wasn't certain how much the deputy believed her own words, but she'd stated them with enough conviction for McHugh that he settled back in his chair and awaited their questions.

Syd took the lead. "How long have you supported a dog park in Serendipity Springs?"

"I formally supported the proposal when it was recently added to the council's agenda."

Syd continued. "Why did you support the measure?"

The dentist blinked once, like he was surprised she would question his position. "Why, uh, it's a good idea."

"Do you own a dog?" Trip asked.

"No, my wife is allergic to pet hair."

"Then it's very civic-minded of you to support the idea," Syd said, "since it won't affect you personally."

"Uh, well, it's the thing to do, isn't it?

"Have your constituents pressured you to support it?" Syd asked.

"Uh, yes."

"Could you describe how they've pressured you?" Trip asked.

"Describe? People have come up to me on the street and told me what a good idea it is."

Thus far, McHugh had not hedged. He'd answered their questions immediately, although he didn't go into any great detail. Syd was buying most of his line, but some sixth sense caused her to wonder if this was the full story. "Do you keep statistics on constituent feedback?" she asked.

"Statistics?" he asked, scrunching up his forehead. "Do I poll the people I represent? No. I usually know if they don't support a particular issue. If I don't hear, I assume everything's okay."

Syd cocked her head to the side. "I'm not sure I understand, Dr. McHugh. First, you said you'd received pressure from constituents to support the dog park, then just now you said you don't hear much if they support a particular issue. Do you have the support of your constituents or not?"

McHugh cleared his throat, threw the bent paper clip to the side. "I've, uh, received both. That's possible, isn't it? A few folks have come up to me on the street and told me they couldn't wait until their dog had a place to run free with other dogs. On the other hand, I've haven't heard anything negative, either from phone calls, letters or emails, to suggest others didn't support the dog park." He picked up the damaged paper clip and began bending and unbending it again, apparently satisfied with his answer.

"At this point," Trip began, "the proposal for a dog park has not been voted on, is that correct?"

McHugh nodded. "Our chair, Avery Wallace, tabled the issue in order to consider it further."

"And as things stand now, you and Councilman Busby support it and Councilmen Brewster and Sheridan oppose it, is that correct?" Trip asked.

"Yes."

"Did Councilman Busby ask you prior to the council discussion whether you supported the proposal or not?"

McHugh didn't respond immediately. "I, uh, don't recall exactly."

"Let me rephrase my husband's question," Syd said. "Did

Councilman Busby ask for your support of the proposal before it came up for discussion?"

The paper-clip bending became more fierce.

"Councilman McHugh?" Deputy Martinez said. "Your response?"

McHugh shifted position as if he'd been thinking and the deputy had brought him out of his trance. "Yes, as I recollect, Busby did ask for my vote. Until then, I'd been neutral."

"What made you switch your support?" Syd asked.

"Because it made sense."

"In what way?" Syd pursued.

McHugh stared directly at her. "In all ways. Is this really important?"

"It is if Councilmen Brewster and Sheridan call you on it," Syd replied. "Or whomever amongst your constituents doesn't support the dog park."

"I don't have to justify my vote on the proposal."

"Really?" Syd continued. "Have you not been cornered by either Brewster or Sheridan? Or Wallace, for that matter, in case she wants to know the basis of your support while she's deciding."

"Even if it should come to that, my opinion is my opinion."

"I see," Syd said, attempting to convey as much disbelief as possible in those two words.

McHugh's dark eyes narrowed. Syd made a note to never become one of his patients or ever get another cavity. She'd hate to see that look over his mask when he was drilling.

"No, I don't think you do, Mrs. Bonner, not that I have to convince you. Like I said earlier, I didn't kill Gordon Kerimides. So my position on the dog park is none of your business."

"Excuse me, Councilman," Trip quickly inserted, "but my wife and I are also your constituents. Your position does matter."

Now it was Trip's turn to be stared at by the councilman. For just a few beats. Suddenly, McHugh's palm came down on his desk. "Okay, okay. I made a deal with Busby. I need at least one council member to approve a variance from the building code, which is preventing me from extending the deck on my home. Satisfied?"

Syd resisted the urge to pat her husband on the back. They'd done it! Not that McHugh had confessed to the murder, but they'd gotten past "a dog park makes good sense" as his only reason for supporting the proposal. Was that it, or was there yet another underlying reason?

She recalled how their PI instructor had described how sometimes revelations from suspects and persons of interest came in layers like onions and had to be peeled away slowly. Perhaps that was the case this time. She also remembered their instructor saying that sometimes after a particularly explosive outburst, the person being interviewed was more likely to reveal things they'd been hiding. Time to pursue that theory. "Since you claim you didn't kill Gordon Kerimides, who do you think did?" she asked.

McHugh blinked several times and cocked his head. "I have no idea. I didn't know the guy. I didn't meet him until Busby and I snuck into their chapel to check out the noise level. Ask Brewster or Sheridan. They're the ones who supported his contention about the noise level."

"You have no other information about possible enemies?" Trip asked.

"Only what I heard from my patients who learned about his opposition to the dog park. I didn't ask them. They volunteered. It's more in the sphere of hearsay, so I didn't pay it much mind."

"And that was ..." Trip continued.

"That he had something going on the side. No one knew what or would say, just that he never left the funeral home. His car was seen there at all hours by anyone who could see the back entrance. Make of that what you will. He may have just felt more comfortable performing his tasks with the dead when he was completely alone."

"Who were these patients?" Syd wanted to know.

He raised his shoulders. "I didn't pay much attention, and by that I mean I'm not holding back. I think one of them lives near the funeral home. Not near where the dog park would be but down the road. I think he or she worked the graveyard shift and saw Kerimides's car there even then." He laughed at his unintentional pun. "I don't know if any of that helps, but it's all I know."

"We appreciate your candor, Councilman. Thank you for your time," Syd said, rising.

Trip picked up on her cue and came to his feet.

Deputy Martinez nodded to McHugh and followed them.

The three didn't speak until they left the building.

"Good interviewing technique, you two. You got him to open up about his real reason for supporting Councilman Busby and at the same time probably eliminated him from the suspect list," Martinez told them.

Trip eyed Syd. "That your conclusion?"

"That final outburst could have been an act. I don't think so, but I'm not a hundred percent sure we got the full story from him." She turned to the deputy. "Thank you for sitting in with us on this one, Deputy Martinez. We may or may not need to interview him again, depending on what our partners find in their interviews."

"I'll wait to hear from you," Martinez said. "In the meantime, apparently the two of you are on my dance card for this afternoon when we meet with Councilman Brewster. I'll see you there."

Twenty minutes later, Syd and Trip were seated at a family restaurant they liked. A sit-down place a notch higher than a fast-food establishment but not quite one with white linen tablecloths. "How does it feel to be back in the saddle again?" Trip asked her once they'd ordered.

"It's been over six months since our last case, and even then, we mainly helped Kat and Rick. So, yes, it feels really good to be interviewing suspects again, or probably in Councilman McHugh's case, persons of interest. And even though we're not done with our PI course yet, more than once today our instructors' words came back to me. Even though we've investigated a number of homicides already, I can tell we'll be even better in the future when we're a professional team."

"You're sounding pretty up, my dear. Does that mean you believe what you told the deputy? That McHugh probably isn't our killer?"

"Pretty much. Not to disparage your interviewing technique, Trip, since that's what finally *tripped* him up, excuse the pun—he didn't have to cave at that point. He could have continued to swear his support was based solely on the dog park being a good idea."

"In other words, it's too soon to celebrate with a chocolate sundae?" He fake-pouted.

"I predict Councilman Sheridan won't be as easy to interview. Order your sundae now."

He scowled. "What makes you think we've got our work cut out for us with the guy? Wasn't he aligned with the victim?"

"Everyone loves pets, right? Especially dogs. Even if they don't have one of their own. Especially if they don't have their own dog. So why is he opposed?"

"Why do you have to make everything so difficult?"

She sat back, offered him a hurt look. "I don't do that! Do I?"

Trip didn't reply. Instead, he picked up his knife and examined it like it was a biology sample.

"You really think that?" she asked.

"Did you not just hear yourself? This guy had no reason for Gordon Kerimides to be dead. So all we have to do is ask him a few questions, let him tell us he didn't kill the guy and we can leave."

She made a face. "Okay, fine. I'll cut back on the dire predictions. Just don't blame me if you begin to wonder about this guy's innocence halfway through the interview."

"You're on, wife! And when we're done in twenty minutes, I'll even look the other way when you come back here for one of their chocolate sundaes to celebrate."

Chapter Nine

"That was Guy. He's been putting together information about dog parks he wants me to review before presenting what he's found to the group," Micki told Kat as they entered a local restaurant. "Would you mind getting lunch on your own? Guy's picking me up outside in a minute."

"Oh, sure. Go on. I'll just order something to go. Update him on our interview with Stacia Kerimides." Kat tried to keep her surprise and skepticism out of her tone. Why would Guy need to rehearse his findings with Micki? As a seasoned attorney, he had no problem speaking to others.

Micki took off to meet Guy, leaving Kat on her own for the first time in weeks. No Rick. No Syd. No Marianne. And most important at the moment, no Micki. She had about an hour and a half before she had to meet Micki and Deputy Martinez to interview Councilman Brewster.

She placed her order and debated how to best use this time on her own. She knew immediately what she wanted to do.

She entered the number for Georgia Julienne on her

phone. "Georgia? I know this is last-minute, but I have a few minutes to come over and view my dress if you're available?"

"As it turns out, yes, I do. Only about forty-five minutes if you get here right away," the dress designer replied.

Kat waited all of two minutes to pick up her order, and then she raced over to Georgia's home/studio on the west side of town. She'd eat later, if there was time.

"No Micki?" Georgia asked.

Thus far, Micki had accompanied Kat on every visit to discuss Kat's wedding dress. Not that Kat didn't appreciate her friend's insight and guidance, but this wasn't Micki's wedding, a point Kat at times struggled to get across to her self-appointed advisor. With the wedding still a while off, the dress was still in development. She'd decided on color, a just barely off-white, which went well with her graying brown hair. The design was evolving. She didn't want anything too revealing or too tight, but she didn't want to appear demure either. She wanted wedding guests but especially Rick to take note that as a senior woman in her sixties, she still maintained a pretty good shape.

"I laid out swatches of several of the fabrics we've discussed in previous meetings," Georgia told her. "If you can't get a good enough feel for any you like, I have full bolts of most of them in my inventory."

Micki had found Georgia when she was doing a story on local fashion. Just turned thirty, the petite artisan was fast gaining a name for herself throughout the state. She received her formal training at the U of Florida while interning for one of the state's main names in fashion design. Since coming to Serendipity Springs, she'd begun a line of ready-to-wear casual clothes aimed at the retiree market, but she'd been more than open to designing for the town's millionaire as a means of supporting her growing retail line.

Even though these swatches now belonged to Kat, she'd washed her hands thoroughly once arriving at Georgia's studio to avoid oil stains from her fingers. It was important that she be able to feel each swatch, finger the intricacies of the laces and touch the smooth satins. So far, she hadn't found anything that both felt good and would look good on her.

"Still nothing?" Georgia asked, coming up to her.

Kat lowered her eyes. "Getting closer. As I've probably told you too many times, I want something traditional and yet chic. None of these has hit me like that."

"I, uh, took the liberty of fleshing out the design that's been evolving from our past discussions. This is by no means final, but I want your reaction."

"Okay, show me." She was ready to see how all her and Micki's ideas translated to paper.

"Actually, I had a little extra time this week, so I did a mock-up. Feel like trying it on?"

Kat's hand went to her heart. "Oh, wow. Yes, of course!" Micki would be so upset she missed this moment. But wait a second; this was her wedding, not Micki's, and thus her moment. She almost ran to the dressing room, her heart beating double time.

"Okay, keep in mind this is just the basic form sewn in muslin. Don't let the feel or color turn you off. This is just to try out the basic style you've been talking about. Unless the fabric you select has to be special-ordered from Europe, we have plenty of time to redo any or all of the design once you've seen how this looks on you."

Although Georgia had removed all the pins, some parts were still held together with basting stitches. Georgia brought the garment down over Kat's head and smoothed it over her body before stepping away so Kat could see herself in the mirror. Though it wasn't too tight, Kat struggled to take a full breath as she stared at herself in a wedding dress for the first time. Well, the first time for real. She was a bride for Halloween when she was five.

Seeing herself clothed all in white was too much. She had to shut her eyes to cut off the effect. Was that really her?

"Well?" Georgia asked expectantly, stepping back into the room.

"I—I don't know what to say, Georgia."

Geogia offered a lilting laugh. "My needy ego will take that as a compliment, although your reaction is typical. Not that my work is always that spellbinding but seeing yourself clothed all in white for the first time can be overpowering. Come out here into the studio so you can see it in real light."

Kat did as directed, taking baby steps so as not to tear anything. She made her way to the three-way mirror across the room to get a better look at herself.

"This is beautiful, Georgia. I can't get over how it feels like a second skin. And moves better than I ever anticipated, and to be truthful, I never gave how it moved with me any thought before now."

"It will feel a tad heavier once it's in the fabric you choose with whatever underlining that requires. Depending on the fabric, it may not have the same flow as this," Georgia told her.

"Okay, I hear you," she said as she pivoted to catch different reflections.

"So much for feel and movement. Let's talk appearance. What do you think of the length? And the amount of fullness in the skirt?"

Oh, yes, the skirt length. Most of their previous sessions had been devoted to this topic. Kat didn't want a train or even a floor length. But she didn't want a miniskirt either. Or short. She was short, and she thought a short skirt would emphasize her height. They'd settled on tea length, but only after Georgia had reassured her it was more a concept than a specific measurement. In the current case, the hem fell about five inches above Kat's ankles.

"You followed my wishes to the letter, but seeing this length on me now, I'd like to change my mind. Can we still do that?" Kat asked.

"No problem," Georgia replied, her voice as smooth and calm as the town's big lake. "If you'll note, the hem is much bigger than it would normally be. If you've got the time, I'll take out the basting and let it down so you can see what it would look like floor-length."

"You've done this before, haven't you? I hope I'm not the first client to keep changing her mind."

Georgia laughed. "It goes with the territory."

Five minutes later, with all the basting removed from the hem, Kat studied her image in the mirror now wearing a floor-length version of the mock-up. "It's so—so—traditional."

Georgia nodded. "Yes? Is that good?"

Tears welled up in Kat's eyes. "My mother would so approve. I wish she was still alive to see her little girl all dressed in white."

"She's here. In spirit. Don't you feel her?"

Kat swiped away the tears now unabashedly rolling down her cheeks. "I can almost envision her standing behind me, nodding her head." She turned to the other woman. "Thanks for understanding."

"I was in your shoes once. It didn't get as far as seeing myself in front of a mirror like you are now, but I still get it."

"I, uh, I'm sorry. What happened, if you don't mind my asking?"

"I don't talk about it much. Let's just say I saved myself from making a terrible decision before it got this far."

"Then I'm happy for you. I was almost a bride once before myself, but I lost my fiancé in a nasty accident. It took a long time to get past that grief. Then I met Rick in this phase of my life and everything changed," Kat said, her tears drying.

"You give me hope that my day will come someday in the future," Georgia said.

"I can't think of anyone more deserving."

"Have you ever had a dog?" Guy asked Micki as they opened their boxes of fried chicken. They'd found a table in a nearby park rather than returning to her condo.

A little heavy for lunch, but Micki was glad he'd gone overboard after her interview with Councilman Busby.

"That's a strange question. Please don't tell me you've been thinking about gifting me with a puppy," she replied.

"That's not a good idea?"

"I've never seen myself as a pet person. I'm not sure they're even allowed in my condo building."

"Not to worry. At least not now. I asked because I've been

learning a lot about dogs and people who own dogs as I've researched dog parks."

"Like what?" she asked.

"Like dogs take a lot more effort than I was aware. My grandpa used to have a few dogs on his farm when I was growing up. If I recall, he put out food once or twice a day, but that was the extent of the care he gave them. Even in heavy rainstorms or winter cold, they stayed outside, although he made a place for them to stay inside the barn when it really got bad.

"But if you own a dog nowadays, you keep them indoors, which means they need to come outdoors several times a day to relieve themselves. At least three, usually four. And if you happen to have a dog within the confines of this town, it has to be on a leash when outside unless kept in a fenced-in area.

"There's more. Here in town they need shots. Not just once. On a periodic basis. And a license. All of that, then there's trips to the groomer, kennel charges if their owner must leave town and finally vet costs, for which a lot of dog owners need health insurance."

"That's a lot," she said. "How does that relate to dog parks?"

"Good question. I guess you could say it's the prelude to the joys and challenges of dog ownership. Imagine going through all that, both the expense and the time, only to learn that your darling has not quite adjusted to living with you. What can you do besides rehome the little pest? Then some well-meaning friend, one who probably doesn't own a dog, suggests all the little guy needs is more exercise and more socialization with other dogs. In other words, the idea of the dog park has emerged as the panacea."

"Is your research saying it's not?" Micki asked, surprised that this topic was becoming more interesting. Was it a candidate for a journalistic piece?

"Not exactly," he replied, finishing his first piece of chicken. "I've only been at this the last day or so. I've visited a park over in Shasta and another in Naranja. Talked to some of the dog owners who were there and got a line on the organizers for both. I've also spent a few hours online browsing various articles."

"What did you learn?" she asked.

"Bottom line? They're great for a dog that needs lots of exercise and doesn't mind getting it in the company of other dogs without attacking them. Got a little dog, shy dog or a sick dog, stay home. Also, make sure the place is big enough and well-maintained, which means you probably will have to pay ongoing fees and will get along best with the other dog owners if there's a clear-cut set of rules everyone buys into. In other words, dog parks are not necessarily the solution for everyone. Anyone who wants to use one, let alone anyone spearheading a drive to establish one, needs to go into the project with open eyes."

"Where does Solomon Ridgedale fall on that spectrum?"

"Not sure. I know he's spoken with Marianne and Beau and Councilman Busby, but have any of them really quizzed him about his dog park knowledge?"

She tried to recall what Marianne and Beau had told the rest of their group of senior sleuths. Their knowledge seemed to start with the assumption that Solomon was on top of his subject. "This isn't good news, Guy. If this murder is directly linked to the dog park, it may have been for nothing, if dog parks aren't all they're cracked up to be."

He tapped her drink cup with his own in a toast. "You're fast, my dear. It sometimes scares me how your brain can take in a few facts and see the big picture so quickly."

"Thanks, but if that's the case, should we all still be involved in this investigation?" she asked.

"Do you want out?" he returned.

"No," she replied without stopping to consider the prospect. "The dog park may somehow be involved in the motive for this murder, but the key point is the murder itself. We've signed on to discover who did it. That part hasn't changed. Still, that doesn't mean we should dismiss what you've learned."

"I was hoping you'd say something like that, although I have to say, I'm not as supportive of Ridgedale as I was two days ago. If he's our culprit, I won't shed as many tears as I might have."

"Even though he's the one who got us started on this case?"

"There is that. His saving grace."

She checked her watch. "Do you want the rest of my french fries? I need to get going to meet Kat and Deputy Martinez. This afternoon we're interviewing Avery Wallace, the only female on the council. Interesting position to be in and so far the only neutral when it comes to the issue of the dog park. How, if at all, does that play into Kerimides's murder?"

Chapter Ten

*M*arianne and Beau checked in with Rick after concluding their interview of Stacia Kerimides. Did he want a report from them now, or did he prefer they all report at the same time once all the first interviews were concluded? Rick suggested they wait but to write down as much as they could recall so they didn't forget later.

"What do you know about Councilman Brewster?" Beau asked as he finished his bowl of chicken noodle soup. He'd actually volunteered to take Mortimer out to the backyard and then fed him when they returned. A satisfied dog now rested under the table at Marianne's feet. Apparently soup wasn't anything for him to get excited about.

"I know as much as you, Beau, which isn't much, other than the man we observed when we attended the council meeting." She pulled up Tad Brewster's public website on her notebook computer. "This says he's forty-seven, single, a graduate of Florida State and a licensed architect."

"That it?"

"He's been on the council for a little over two years and

cites his hobbies as cooking and film noir movies. Maybe we can compare recipes? Kidding."

Beau pulled her notebook closer to read it himself. "Architect, huh? I wonder how that figures in his position against the dog park."

"Kind of a moot point now," she replied. "We don't need him to justify his position on that issue unless it directly relates to the Kerimides murder."

"In other words," he said, "we focus on that relationship, if there even was one."

"I'm as concerned about working with Deputy Hastings as interviewing Brewster," she said. "Have you worked with him before?"

"Just enough to say hello. Seemed like a nice guy. Upright. Loyal to Rick and, I'm guessing, now loyal to Sheriff Quinn."

Since Brewster worked from his home, Hastings had suggested they meet first at a coffee shop a few blocks away from there.

"Thanks for meeting me here," Deputy Hastings said, rising from the table he'd picked for them.

Okay, he was polite. One point for him. Would she feel the same way about him once they'd concluded their interview? Or even sooner, since he apparently had a reason for meeting them prior to meeting Brewster?

Hastings offered to get them coffee, which they both declined. "I'll be brief about wanting to meet with you before we talk with the councilman. Cards on the table, I'm not the least bit crazy about the two of you being involved in this investigation. I respected Rick Formero as sheriff and now Sheriff Quinn. That's the only reason I'm going along with this plan. I'll do the introductions, and I'll monitor your questions. If you wander too far astray from department policy, I'll end the interview, whether you think you're finished or not. Do I make myself clear?"

What had Rick agreed to, allowing this young man to oversee their interview? She kicked herself mentally for not checking in with Kat and Micki to get their impression of him before she and Beau met him. Too late now. They didn't have much chance but to do their best to get along with him.

"Perfectly," she replied.

"What she said," Beau echoed.

Tad Brewster lived in the newest part of town, on the outskirts, actually. His home was a one-story ranch with an attached triple garage. Three-fourths of the front was black and appeared to have been produced by the method she'd seen on one of the home design shows she watched, where just the surface of the wood was burned.

Brewster greeted them at the front door. "Come in, come in. I thought we could meet in my office downstairs. It's just off my studio." He didn't look directly at Marianne or Beau but instead focused on Hastings.

They followed him down stairs guarded with a clear acrylic railing. At first, the bottom floor appeared to be a totally open plan. An entire wall of windows overlooked a green lawn with a pond at one end. Bookcases took up the entire opposite wall. A long table with a white surface occupied most of the space in front of them. It was completely empty as compared to a large wooden desk on the other side in front of the windows, which was stacked with piles of architectural magazines and file folders. A drawing easel took up the rest of the room.

All that flashed by as he led them into an interior room

with a large for-show desk, huge olive-green leather office chair and two smaller visitor chairs on the other side of the desk. "I, uh, didn't know there'd be three of you. I'll get another chair from the studio," Brewster said.

"No need," Hastings replied. "I'll stand." He then went on to introduce Marianne and Beau and explain why they had accompanied him.

Brewster slipped into the main chair, leaned back, started to place a foot on top of the desk, then reconsidering, withdrew it. "You want to talk about the Kerimides murder. Okay, I'll answer whatever you want to know, but that won't be much. But I'll start by saying I didn't kill him."

"You didn't know the man?" Marianne began, ignoring his last comment.

"Not well. He contacted me a while back when word of the projected site of the dog park got around. Insisted the council scrap the idea posthaste."

"Is that when you became opposed to the idea?" Beau asked.

"Around then. The concept had been floating around for a while, but nothing serious had been done about it."

"Why did you oppose installing a dog park in town?" she asked. So much for avoiding the subject of the dog park and focusing on Kerimides, but since he'd said he hadn't known the man well, there didn't appear to be much else she could ask.

"It's not that I don't like dogs. I just don't feel the community owes their owners the large amount of space and money required to maintain a park just for canines."

"Oh? Then if some well-meaning benefactor donated

land and a trust fund to pay for maintenance, you'd be okay with a private venture?" she asked.

Beau's eyes were shooting darts her direction. Right, it was a little off-topic, but she wanted to get him talking, about anything if she could, so she could distract him enough to get back to the subject of the murder victim.

"I, uh, I don't have an answer for you, Mrs. Putnam. That situation hasn't arisen."

"Let's go back to what you said about Kerimides contacting you about the dog park," Beau said. "Could you describe the circumstances in which that happened?"

"There's not much to describe. He called me and asked for my help in preventing the dog park from becoming a reality."

"Did you agree immediately?" Marianne asked.

"No, of course not, but I felt it was my duty to hear him out."

"How did you do that?" she pursued.

"We exchanged several emails. I asked him to lay out his reasons for objecting to the proposed dog park. He replied within a day, citing the noise factor, which he'd already referred to in his first contact with me. I then asked him to be more specific about his noise concerns, which he did in his next email."

"Did you ever meet him in person?" Beau asked.

"A few times. Before I did, I sniffed out my fellow council members to assess their positions on the issue. When I learned that Dan Sheridan was not convinced it was a good idea, I got him to meet Kerimides with me for coffee. A few days later, Kerimides gave us a tour of the public parts of the funeral home so we could get a feel for the potential noise ourselves. Then the day before the council was to debate the proposal, we met with him again to make sure we got our facts straight."

"How would you describe the man?" Marianne asked.

Brewster sat forward, staring at her like she'd asked her question in a foreign language. "Excuse me? I'm not sure what you mean."

Had she stumped him? If so, how? "We never met the man, other than seeing him in the audience of the council meeting we attended. We're trying to get a feel for what there was about him that prompted someone to take his life."

"Oh." He sounded relieved. "For a guy who works so much on his own, you know, dealing with the remains of the dead, I found him to be very personable. He treated Dan and me with respect and gave us as much time as we needed to learn more about his concerns."

Having established a little about Kerimides's personality, Marianne dug further. "Can you think of anyone who would want to kill him?"

Brewster paused for just a beat before answering. "No. Perhaps someone who felt their loved one's remains weren't dealt with appropriately. Or maybe"—he paused dramatically, as if debating whether to proceed—"the guy who's so determined to build the dog park. Ridgemon, no, Ridgedale. Solomon Ridgedale. He was pretty charged up during and following the council meeting where the dog park was discussed, but I can't see him knocking Gordon off just for that."

Gordon? Apparently Brewster had gotten to know the man enough to use his first name.

Beau raised a brow her direction, questioning whether

they were done. She nodded imperceptibly. "One last question, Councilman. Where were you the other night between ten and six in the morning?"

"That was when he was supposed to have been killed? I was here that entire time. Alone, although I was on the phone around nine thirty with a client. I can give you his name, if you want."

"Or we can check your phone," Marianne said.

He retrieved his phone from the top of his desk and handed it to her. "Be my guest."

"I'll do that part," Hastings said. He hadn't appeared to be actively engaged in this interview, but apparently he was.

Hastings scrolled through several entries on Brewster's phone before replying. "He's right. There's an entry here that started at nine twenty-eight that night and ran until nine fifty-six. Nothing more until eight fourteen the next morning."

"You're welcome to pull the phone records for the weeks preceding his death. You'll find the time either I contacted him or he got in touch with me. They should match what I've already told you."

"Thanks. We will," Hastings said.

They'd covered most of the questions Marianne and Beau had planned to ask, but Marianne had a feeling there was something more. But at the moment, she couldn't think what it was.

They thanked Brewster for his time, left their contact information and filed upstairs and out to their respective vehicles.

"Hope you got all you needed," Hastings said, following them to their car, "because my schedule is filling up fast sitting in with your other friends."

"For now, Deputy," Beau replied, checking Marianne with his eyes.

Marianne didn't add anything, since she hadn't formed any specific ideas about what she thought was missing as it related to Brewster.

They'd turned to get into their car when Hastings spoke again. "Is this how it's gonna be now that Rick is setting up his own PI business?"

"You mean the sheriff's department teaming up with people you consider unqualified to investigate homicides?" Marianne replied, cutting to the real issue.

Hastings bit a lip. "I didn't say that exactly, Mrs. Putnam. But to be honest, it's my opinion the sheriff's department could solve things quicker without the extra help."

"We're sorry you feel that way," Beau answered before Marianne had a chance to say anything more incriminating. "Perhaps by the time we've helped wrap this case, you'll have changed your mind about us?"

"We'll see, Mr. Putnam." Hastings pivoted and headed for his own vehicle.

"He doesn't mince words, does he?" Marianne said to Beau as she opened her own door.

"Picture us if the circumstances were reversed. Wouldn't you feel threatened?"

"I'd like to think I'd be happy for the help, but I get your point. If I'm honest with myself, I'd probably be telling him something similar. If not worse."

"Then we have our assignment," Beau said. "You and I have to gather the troops, up our game and prove that guy wrong."

Chapter Eleven

"So we meet again, Deputy Martinez," Trip said, his businessman persona coming through. "I thought our first interview combining our respective talents went pretty well."

"Yes," Martinez replied guardedly. "I appreciate your sticking within the guidelines I gave you."

"What can you tell us about our next interviewee, Councilman Sheridan?" Syd asked.

"Not much. I assumed you were doing the initial research on him. I've never met him."

"We have. He has two websites. One for being on the council and the other as a management professor at the community college. He's divorced, two children. He was born in North Carolina and came to Serendipity Springs ten years ago. Do you know anything more than that?"

"The divorce happened since he moved here. Apparently his former wife didn't want to leave their home in North Carolina. She was born and grew up there. She had trouble fitting into our local scene." Martinez stopped and seemed to consider what she'd just told them. "That's basically hearsay.

I heard it from a friend who works at a local restaurant. The wife, Janelle, confided in her before she left town. The marriage had been in trouble before that. He was very close to his mother, who'd been the one to encourage him to leave North Carolina, even though she'd been content to remain there on her own."

"Thanks," Syd said. "That gives us a little something to go on."

"You're okay meeting him in the park and not his home?" Martinez asked. "He needs to be on campus later but doesn't want to be seen by his students being questioned by the authorities. And his apartment is too far from campus to make it back to his class on time."

MacKinnon Park was located about three blocks from campus, far enough away that students and other college personnel wouldn't see one of their own. It circumnavigated a small lake, reservoir actually. A few picnic tables were clustered together at one end. Not too close to the water, in case a hungry gator came calling. Dan Sheridan, who'd arrived first, had selected the table farthest from the water.

Martinez did the honors, introducing Syd and Trip and explaining their presence.

"I've read about this phenomenon," Sheridan said once she'd finished. "I guess non-law-enforcement consultants are not all that unusual. Interesting way for the sheriff's department to interact in the name of community relations."

Trip nodded. "Yes, that's one way of looking at it."

"Also provides the authorities with a scapegoat should things go sour," Sheridan added, watching all three of them for their reactions.

Martinez opened her mouth to say something, but Trip

got there first. "True. I suppose that could happen, but my wife and I are confident we've established a relationship with the sheriff based on mutual trust."

"Good. Glad to hear that. So? What can I help you with? And before we get into your questions, let's start with me saying I didn't kill the man or know who did."

The man was direct. She had to give him that. She and Trip could take the same tack. "Since you chose to begin with stating your innocence, let's explore that first," Syd said. "Where were you two nights ago between ten in the evening and eight the next morning?"

"I presume that's the time of death? What is my alibi? I was out celebrating the birthday of one of the other professors until about eleven thirty. After that, I returned to my condo, alone, and went to bed until seven thirty the next morning. And no, there was no one there waiting for me. I didn't make any phone calls during that time, except I waited up until midnight to play Wordle. You can find that on my phone, although I guess that wouldn't prove where I was."

"How well did you know Gordon Kerimides?" Trip asked.

"Not well, but I did know him before this dog park thing came up. He helped me through a very difficult time in my life. My mother was killed in a terrible car crash when she was traveling in Europe six years ago. I'd been divorced about two years at that point. My ex-wife had moved back to North Carolina, where we'd both grown up. Our two kids were both in college on the West Coast. I was on my own making arrangements and had no idea what to do. I called the local funeral home and wound up speaking with Gordon.

"He had this manner about him that immediately calmed me. He took over most of the administrative details required to bring her back to the States and then to put her to rest. To be frank, her remains were a mess. I was never able to see her body, but he realized I needed closure and helped me do that.

"I haven't really seen him since then, although I've attended a few funerals at the funeral home. I guess he wasn't much of a social animal, so I never ran into him around town. It was only when this dog park issue arose that our paths crossed again."

"Let's talk about that," Syd said after he'd finished his piece. "You have gone on record as not supporting the dog park. How did that happen?" Good, nice, open-ended question.

"It's not that I don't like dogs, although I don't own one. My ex was allergic to them, or so she claimed, so we never had any around. You'd think getting a dog of my own would've been one of the first things I did after our divorce, but I was deep into teaching a new management class that semester and my mind was elsewhere. The idea of installing a city dog park has been kicking around the council ever since I became part of it three years ago, but it only took on serious tones this past year. I attribute that to the Ridgedale guy, who's been spearheading the effort.

"He approached me several months ago, asking for my support. I didn't say yes but did tell him I'd look into the issue. I must have asked Tad Brewster in passing at one of the council meetings what he thought of the idea, and he filled me in. By then, the specific city land to be used had become public knowledge. When he told me that Kerimides was opposed to that particular spot being selected, I threw my support to him. I'm sure there are other suitable spots in town for a dog park, but this one was problematic for Kerimides.”

“In other words,” Trip filled in, “your non-support of the current proposal was based on your support for Kerimides. And only on that?”

“That’s putting it a bit bluntly, but essentially, yes.”

Syd wanted so much to continue this part of the discussion, the concept of “you scratch my back, I’ll scratch yours,” but they weren’t here to discuss Sheridan’s personal ethics, unless they related to him being the murderer. Instead, she returned to his first statement. “You said you didn’t know who murdered Kerimides. Maybe you don’t know, but is there anyone you suspect?”

“That’s your job, isn’t it?”

“Our job is to question everyone who had something to do with the victim and gather their thoughts about likely suspects,” Trip told him.

Sheridan was quiet for several beats. He pulled at the collar of his light blue golf shirt. Back in the day, her professors wore suits or at least sport jackets. “Have you questioned Brewster yet?” he asked at last.

“He’s on our associates’ list,” Syd replied. “What do you think he might be telling us?”

Sheridan thought a bit about his answer. “It’s possible he knew Kerimides before this dog park thing happened.”

Syd pounced. “Knew him? How?”

Sheridan held up a cautionary hand. “I’m not saying he actually did know the guy, just suggesting he be asked.”

“Based on what?” Trip asked.

“I overheard a couple telephone exchanges when our meetings were temporarily paused. I never heard him say

'Gordon' or 'Kerimides,' but I did hear a few references to 'services' and 'the deceased.' Not enough for me to claim it definitely was Kerimides on the other end but enough for me to be suspicious."

"When did those calls take place?" Syd asked.

"I'd have to go back through my council minutes to give you exact dates, but at least six months ago if not more."

"That was before the dog park proposal heated up, wasn't it?" Syd asked.

"Yes." He hesitated as if there was still more to say, if he decided to do so. He licked his lips, then seemed to make a decision. "At the risk of sounding like a gossip, I have to add that his tone with whoever was on the other end of the line was ... friendly."

He seemed to want them to follow up rather than say anything else himself. "Intimate?" Syd asked, thinking she'd gone too far. But she had to ask.

"That's too strong. I couldn't think of a word that means friendlier than friendly."

She couldn't wait to find out what Marianne and Beau had learned from Tad Brewster. How would he have described his relationship with the deceased? "Can you recall anything else he said in those exchanges?"

"Not that he said, but once, he noticed me attempting to appear like I wasn't listening when I was. He rose immediately and left the room, still on his phone."

"Did either of you comment on his calls after he'd hung up?" Trip asked.

"Only once. He said, 'Sorry. Nervous client,' as if that explained it all."

"And you never asked about them?" Syd asked, determined not to let this topic go until it ran out of steam.

"We may be making too much of this," Sheridan said. "It's not like Brewster and I are buds. We're different people and not friends."

Apparently the steam was already gone. Time to wrap things up.

Syd and Trip both thanked the man for his time. They walked with Martinez back to her vehicle. "Even though we didn't interview Councilman Brewster, can we subpoena his phone records?" Syd asked her. "I'd like to know more about those phone calls Sheridan thought might have been exchanged with Kerimides."

"I'll look into it and get back to you," Martinez replied. "Other than that, did you hear anything that might lead you to believe Councilman Sheridan is a likely suspect?"

"I was interested to learn that Kerimides had helped him in the past," Syd said. "So far, most of what we've heard about the victim hasn't been positive."

"But don't forget," Trip pointed out, "Sheridan only opposed the dog park proposal because of his own positive feelings about him."

"Not surprising, since I suspect that kind of thing happens more frequently than we, the public, are aware," Syd said. "But I was surprised that he admitted as much."

"Are we done here?" Martinez asked, cutting off further discussion that involved her. Why was that? Was the deputy trying to remain neutral out of loyalty to her boss, or did she not share their opinions? Something to think about later. Martinez appeared anxious to get going.

"I'll check with Sheriff Quinn about Councilman Brewster's phone records, but don't plan on it yet. Subpoenaing a council member's private phone records could be a touchy subject," Martinez told them before she took off.

"Do you think it's possible that Brewster had a stronger relationship with Kerimides than we've been led to believe?" Trip asked Syd once they were alone.

"It never would have occurred to me until Sheridan brought it up. That's telling as well. He was trying to redirect our attention to another council member away from himself."

"By 'telling,' do you mean you think that Sheridan was hiding something?"

"I don't know right now. Maybe if we get to see Brewster's phone records we'll learn more, one way or the other."

Chapter Twelve

Stacia Kerimides asked that their custodian, Billy Sampson, not be interviewed until the end of his day. So Marianne and Beau interviewed Warren Meek, the funeral director, first. Stacia had reserved one of the small conference rooms that were used for dealing with bereaved families for these interviews.

Marianne had pictured a tall, thin, dour Ichabod Crane type, perhaps because of his connection with death in Washington Irving's story. Meek was more the Jolly Green Giant type. Tall, yes, but he also had a full head of Beach Boys blond hair and a scruffy blondish-red beard. And he was at least twenty pounds overweight.

"This is a quiet week for services," Meek said. "I didn't have anything scheduled today. I came in just for this interview. I probably knew Gordon better than most, with the exception of Stacia. Although that's not saying much, because Gordon and I weren't friends or anything even close to that."

Once again, Martinez explained her presence and the reason why the Putnams were there. Then she turned the meeting over to them.

Marianne began with the opening Meek had provided. "You said you probably knew Mr. Kerimides better than most. Could you describe what you meant by that?"

"I'm a certified funeral director. I'm also an ordained minister. Early in my ministerial career I found that having my own church wasn't for me; conducting services, counseling the families and more or less being the public face of this funeral home work better. I also fill in at various congregations around town when a last-minute substitute preacher is needed. But enough of my background, other than to say I know my place in this funeral home. I'm not a mortician nor an administrator. I do my thing, and I stayed out of Gordon and Stacia's way with their jobs."

"Okay," Beau said, "where are you going with that?"

"It means there have been days when I haven't run into either of them. The only times I did see them were when clients wanted the body laid out or treated a special way; I got in touch with Gordon. Other times, they had questions about billing or scheduling, things like that. That's when I would check in with Stacia."

"Based on the times you did see him, how would you describe the man?" Beau asked.

"I've been going back through my memory bank about that, thinking that was the kind of thing you'd ask me. I've only known Gordon since I was hired for this position, and that was after his brother's supposed death. Before that, all three of them, Gordon, his brother, Tom, and Stacia, shared all duties, although I guess Stacia wound up doing most of the funerals and handling the day-to-day administrative stuff. When Tom disappeared, Gordon decided to bring in a full-time person to handle the services and assumed Stacia would continue being administrator.

"In other words, Gordon enjoyed the undertaking part and jealously guarded his role in it. Stacia is also trained to prepare the bodies, but I've never seen her allowed to do it. Instead, Gordon found this guy who lives in Shasta who's willing to come in on an *ad hoc* basis and cover for him when needed.

"When I say 'guarded,' I'm serious. No one except the company he hired to dispose of the human waste was allowed to enter the embalming quarters. Talk to Billy about that one. He was nearly fired on the spot when he first started working here because he had the audacity to clean in there one day. I asked Kerimides once why the attitude and got the brush-off. The only thing he'd say was that he was a very private person and preferred to be left alone when he was dealing with the deceased. That was as close as he got to an apology. As close as he got to acting human, for that matter."

"Tell us more about his being a 'private person,'" Marianne said.

"For starters, I rarely saw him interact with anyone. Stacia, sometimes, but that was usually when there was some issue they both had to address. On those occasions, he didn't treat her as an equal or even as a relative. He wasn't an angry person. In fact, if pressed, I'd say he was unemotional. Not quite robotic but certainly not friendly."

"You said he told you he was a private person," Beau said. "Did he say why that was?"

"Funny you should ask," Meek replied. "An hour or so after he gave me the brush-off when I asked what had made him such a private person, he returned to explain that he was used to doing everything with his brother. They'd even become morticians together. Since his brother's disappearance, he hadn't found anyone else he could depend on. He only told me that once. Guess he felt he didn't need to repeat himself."

"Did he ever refer to his brother's disappearance?" Marianne wanted to know.

Meek wrinkled his forehead. "Give me a minute to think about that. I know something was said about Tom Kerimides at least once, but it could have been Stacia who said it. Now I remember. It was Gordon. He didn't attend my services very often, but sometime during my first few months on the job I looked up to see him in the back row. Afterwards, he explained that the deceased had been the principal at the junior high school he and his brother attended in Shasta. Then he complimented me for the way I'd incorporated ideas suggested by several former students for my comments. He added that his brother would have been even more impressed because he worked in the school office one year. He shook his head then and murmured, 'So much he's missed,' more to himself than to me."

Beau cocked his head, attempting to understand that last comment. "Funny. I got the impression from Stacia Kerimides that there was bad blood between the brothers. She even hinted that Gordon was somehow behind Tom's disappearance."

Meek pulled his chair away from the conference table. "I should have realized she'd tell you about her suspicions." Pause. "Yes, from what I've observed, the relationship between Gordon and Stacia hasn't been amicable. Not that they fought, they just kept their distance from each other.

Stacia is a full-fledged mortician. She has been trained to do all the tasks Gordon did. But he wouldn't let her. Don't know why, and he never explained.

"Every once in a while, something would come up requiring a special tweak to the service or to the handling of the remains, and she would say something like, 'Tom would never have done it that way.' Then she'd refer to the infamous fishing trip the brothers had taken and how only Gordon had come back. 'He went from being one-third owner to half-owner who runs this place like he thinks he owns it all,' she said. 'Tom never should have trusted him to go on that boat trip.' She volunteered all that. I never asked. Nor did I follow up when she'd make such statements.

"She was right about Gordon running the place like he was the sole owner. Although she was the one who hired me, she came across as taking orders from him. It was only later that I learned she was part owner."

"But you never followed up when she told you those things?" Marianne asked.

Meek folded his hands and leaned into the table. "I'm an ordained minister, Mrs. Putnam. I couldn't let such profound statements go by without attempting to minister to the needs of the speaker. She's still grieving the loss of her husband, even though it's been years since he disappeared. Probably because she's never had closure. Her life seems to still be in limbo. It's no wonder Gordon was able to take charge."

She wasn't sure what to make of this man. He would have had them believe Kerimides sincerely missed his brother until Trip called him on it. Then under the guise of his ministerial calling, Meek admitted how much more he'd learned about the missing brother from his wife. He seemed to be playing both sides of the street. Was that to keep his job? Especially now that Gordon was gone.

Time to change topics. "Who do you think killed him?" she asked.

"I wasn't hinting that Stacia murdered him," Meek quickly replied. "I was just answering your question about her."

"Well, someone killed him," Beau said. "I don't know how many details you know, but it wasn't pretty. Who would do that?"

Meek didn't respond for several beats.

"Warren?" Beau pushed. "Other than his sister-in-law, you're around here the most. You may not know, but surely you have your suspicions?"

Meek rubbed the front of one thumb with the pad of the other, staring at his hands like the answer was there. Finally, he spoke. "Yes, I am around here a lot but not as much as the other two. Perhaps you should look there."

"Are you referring to the custodian, Billy Sampson?" Beau asked.

"He is the only other staff person around here," Marianne said.

"Unlike me, Sampson is here every day, and he has access to the entire building with the exception of the embalming room. The two of us don't talk much, so I don't know anything about him. I'm just speaking about access."

"Thanks," Beau replied. "Anything else you could add?"

"No. I didn't expect to reveal this much."

They did the usual spiel about calling them if he thought of anything else and dismissed him.

"Except for getting us started with Meek, you didn't say

anything, Deputy Martinez. Does that mean you're coming to accept our participation on the case?" Marianne asked.

Before answering, Martinez opened her large bag, took out a thermos and poured herself a cup of coffee. "Want some? There are some extra cups across the room."

"No, thanks," Marianne said for both of them.

Martinez sipped her coffee. "I didn't speak because there was no reason to. You both seem to understand your boundaries and are staying within them."

Considering the need for coffee and her hesitation, the admission must be difficult for her. "Thank you."

Martinez checked her watch. "The custodian, Sampson, should be here soon. I saw restrooms down the hall in case you need one."

"I'm fine," Beau replied.

"Me, too," Marianne added.

They waited. In silence. Fortunately, Sampson showed up within minutes. Wearing one-piece blue denim overalls, Billy Sampson looked to be about five seven, somewhere in his thirties to fifties, with scraggly red hair that touched his collar. The most notable feature of his face was a large mole to the left of his mouth.

Martinez did her intro thing, even offering him some of her coffee, which he, too, declined. Once he sat, he bit a fingernail, then stopped as soon as he seemed to realize what he was doing. "Not sure what I can tell you. Mrs. Kerimides is the one who found the body."

"Yes, we're aware of that," Marianne said. "We've already talked to Mrs. Kerimides, and we've even seen the room where she found his body. We need more background information from you."

"Background information?" The phrase seemed to throw him.

"We'd like to ask you some questions, that's all," Beau told him.

"O-okay?" Sampson replied, not quite following.

"How long have you worked here, Billy?" Marianne asked.

"Uh, ten years or so, I guess. I was here before the other Kerimides, Tom, the brother, disappeared."

"What are your job duties?" Beau asked.

"Everything required to keep the place clean," Billy answered.

"Could you be more specific?" Marianne asked.

"I sweep the floors, vacuum the carpet, take out trash. Sometimes I wash the windows, although Mrs. K calls a company to do the outside ones. That what you wanted to know?"

"Exactly," Beau said. "Where do you perform all those tasks?"

"In the building," Billy replied, like he couldn't understand why that wasn't obvious.

"The entire building?" Marianne asked. They knew the answer but wanted to hear his version.

"Yeah, well, everything except where Mr. K worked on all the bodies."

Beau followed up. "Why was that? Didn't that room get dirty also?"

The custodian shrugged. "Guess so. I was only there once. The first day on the job. No one told me it was off-limits, but as soon as I went in, Mr. K had a fit. Told me to get out immediately and never to clean that room or any of the rooms next to it again."

"Did he tell you why?" Beau asked.

"Said I could hurt myself with all the chemicals in the room. Didn't have to tell me twice. I've avoided that area ever since."

"Ever see anyone else go in there?" Marianne asked.

"Just the guy who subs for him. Doesn't happen often, but even Mr. K got sick sometimes."

"How about Mrs. K?" she asked, using Billy's name for Stacia.

"Oh, no! Every so often, he'd remind me that she was not to go anywhere near the body room."

"What about disposal of the, uh, aftermath of the embalming?" Beau asked. "How was that handled?"

"Oh, yeah," Billy said. "Forgot about that. Probably because I wasn't usually around when the guy came."

"The guy?" Marianne repeated. This must be the person Meek had referred to.

"That's all I know of him, other than he exists. I wasn't supposed to lock the outside door near the body area on weekdays until I came in the next morning. He's from some company that does that sort of thing." He shivered. "Ugh. Not something I'd want to do."

Although she could agree with him on that point, it seemed an ironic statement for a guy who cleaned everywhere else in the facility where death was present.

"Talk to Mrs. K about that one," Billy offered. "She'd have the bills from whoever it is."

Maybe. Stacia said that Kerimides had handled the finances where the embalming area was concerned. Is that why she hadn't mentioned this outside company? Or had she deliberately sidestepped the subject? A second interview with the sister-in-law was definitely needed.

Marianne glanced at Beau, telegraphing whether they were done.

Beau still had questions. "You said you didn't find the body, but we understand you came almost immediately when you heard Mrs. Kerimides screaming. What did you find when you got there?"

Billy scrunched up his eyes. "Find? The same thing Mrs. K did, Mr. K's body. Dead. He was obviously dead."

"Did you check to make sure?" Beau asked.

"You mean feel for a pulse? No. It was obvious. His eyes stared straight ahead. His skin had a different color."

"What did you do?" Marianne pursued. Either Billy was being cagey about the death scene, or he had no idea how his first-on-scene perspective might be of help.

"At first I gagged. I may work around the dead all the time, but it's not like I actually see them, especially see someone I work for. Meanwhile, Mrs. K just stood there staring at him until finally she told me to call the sheriff's office. Which I did. Should've done that immediately. Guess I was in shock. When I hung up, she was still standing there, the color gone out of her, too. I found a chair and made her sit down.

"I got her some water, then went to let the sheriff's people in. They both went directly to Mr. K's body, then one of them called someone else. Must've been the guys who took away the body after they photographed everything in sight.

"They brought me into this room to get my story. I thought I'd finished until I got the message you wanted to talk to me today."

"It's always important to capture an eyewitness's initial reaction to a traumatic event like Mr. Kerimides's murder," Marianne told him. "But it's not unusual for witnesses to be interviewed a second time or more after they've had time to get past the initial shock and process what they saw. That's why we're here."

"Oh," was his only reply.

After asking for his alibi for the estimated time of the murder—he was home asleep—they thanked him for his time and shared their contact information.

"Thanks for all your help today," Beau said to Martinez as they were making ready to leave.

"Let's call it a day," Marianne said, "but we'd like to visit with Stacia Kerimides one more time. Perhaps tomorrow?"

"I'll check with Sheriff Quinn and let you know," Martinez replied noncommittally.

"Deputy Martinez seems a little more cooperative than earlier," Beau said. "Have we made a new friend?" he asked Marianne once it was just the two of them.

"Always the optimist," she replied. "How about we go home and crash for an hour or so before we have to meet the others at Kat's? I'm exhausted."

"Are you saying this routine is a little much for our aging bodies?"

"Shut your mouth! We don't want Rick or the others getting the slightest idea we may be out of our element. We'll learn from our experience today and modify as needed," she said.

"Now who's the optimist?" he asked.

She stopped in her tracks. "Seriously, Beau. Are you having second thoughts about becoming part of Rick's team?"

"No, not at all," he returned, opening the door for her. "You've done this more than me. I signed up because I didn't want to be left out. Not the best of reasons, I know. But after today, I feel energized. The interview part of this job is fascinating. I hadn't realized how much depended on the interviewer's questioning skills. I learned a lot just listening to you."

She looked back at him. "Thanks. That means a lot."

"I do have one more question for you."

"What's that?"

"Would you consider ordering out tonight?

Chapter Thirteen

Once again, Micki was Kat's passenger as they drove to Avery Wallace's art gallery near the heart of downtown Serendipity Springs.

"How was your lunch?" Micki asked.

Sounded like an innocent inquiry, but Kat sensed Micki had something else in mind.

"You heard that I went to get a progress update from Georgia, didn't you?"

"I called her for the same thing. You must have left her studio just minutes before I checked in with her. She said you were nearing a decision on some of the design features and narrowing your fabric choices."

"You're okay with my going to see her on my own, I hope?"

"Uh, sure," Micki replied a little too slowly. "I was just surprised, that's all."

"Please don't take this the wrong way, Mick. I really appreciate all you're doing to help me get ready for the wedding, but I've been having so much trouble deciding what I want, I thought if it was just me, this once, maybe I could clear my brain and see things more clearly."

"My presence confuses you?"

So much for trying to be diplomatic. "Not exactly. But you have so many ideas, great ideas, that I have to run to keep up. I wanted things to slow down."

"Slow down? You do realize the clock is ticking? One of these days you have to make a decision."

"Yes. It may not seem that way, but I do. And I repeat, I really appreciate your help."

"Okay, I get that. You're welcome. But here's a thought. You probably don't expect to hear it coming from me, but there is no such thing as the perfect wedding dress. The perfect part will come from wearing it to marry Rick."

Kat played that idea through her brain as they made their way down the next block. Imagine Micki admitting there was no perfect dress. "Thanks. I hadn't thought about it that way."

"Let's you and I have coffee together once we've gotten past this investigation. Rather than my asking you, 'Do you want this or that,' I want you to describe your dream dress to me. I think it's locked away somewhere in your head, and we just need to encourage that vision to emerge."

Kat considered that idea. "That's not a bad idea. Let's get through this last interview today and maybe the next few days, and then we'll talk."

"Speaking of which, how do you want to handle Avery Wallace?"

"Frankly, I haven't given her role in this murder much thought," Kat said. "She seems to be the voice of reason on the council."

"Or she's afraid to take a stand," Micki replied. "Pardon my negativity."

"Have you ever been to her gallery?"

"Last year sometime. I was considering an article on the local art scene, looking for a new angle. I hoped she'd be able to help."

"And?" Kat asked.

"She claimed she was preoccupied with studying upcoming council business and begged off. Told me she'd be happy to consider whatever ideas I wanted to bounce off her. In my opinion, for someone in the creative market, she wasn't very creative herself. I hope I got the wrong impression, but we'll see."

"Before this Kerimides murder, Syd had suggested the two of us take in this gallery to search for a few pieces for the ranch house. It'll be difficult not to sneak a few peeks at her walls while we're there."

Micki chuckled. "Knowing you, you'll stick to your guns and deprive yourself of even a few brief seconds of enjoyment."

"Well, I'll try." She laughed. "But despite your high expectations of me, I'm no saint. I just won't buy anything today."

Deputy Colin Hastings pulled up at the gallery at the same time they did. He remained in his vehicle a few seconds to finish up what appeared to be a can of cola. Reenergizing for his next go-round with them?

He approached with a stoic demeanor. "Ladies? Just so you know, this is the only day I've been scheduled to babysit, uh, assist you, so you probably want to get as much from Ms. Wallace as you can today."

Even though he'd corrected himself, he probably did

think all he'd been doing today was *babysitting* these wannabe detectives. Only his remaining loyalty to Rick stopped him from saying more. It had to have been a tough year for him with all the changes that had occurred in the sheriff's office. First Rick lost the election. Then Rick's successor turned out to be crooked and got himself killed. Now, after thinking his work life had finally righted itself, his new boss assigned him to a group he must consider rank amateurs.

"Okay, Deputy, thanks for letting us know," Kat replied. No need to tell him that if they needed to do second interviews, he'd still be their boy.

Avery Wallace's gallery, Articipation, occupied the corner of the street that included a restaurant, a high-end shoe store and a bookstore. Kat had expected muted walls, most likely an off-white. Surprise. Black. The lighting, a masterpiece, exuded an air of mystery without being sinister or gloomy.

Though they'd not heard a bell announce their presence, Avery Wallace stood waiting for them in an interior doorway. She was a tall, slender woman in her early forties. Straight blond hair hung to her shoulders. Though Kat had pictured someone draped in a bright caftan to signify her artsy leanings, Avery Wallace wore a cream-colored cropped sweater and tight cream-colored pants. "Welcome to Articipation," she said evenly.

Deputy Hastings sprang into action, once again explaining their presence.

"I thought we could meet in my office," Wallace told them. "I'll bring in an extra chair so all three of you can sit."

"That won't be necessary, Ms. Wallace," Hastings said.

That didn't stop Avery Wallace. "Please, sit, all of you,"

she told them when she returned with an extra chair. She took the lead as soon as the trio was seated. "I've set aside time to speak with you, although I have a client coming in soon. That shouldn't be a problem, since I don't have much to contribute to your investigation. I never met the man. Funeral homes tend to steer away from the type of art I deal in."

"That's interesting," Kat replied. "I'd think you would have run into each other at various community events, since you are ... were both businesspeople."

"Gordon Kerimides left that part of the business, schmoozing community leaders, to his sister-in-law, Stacia. I've met her a few times. Although I guess her role wasn't so much to sell the business as to reassure the community they were safe and could be trusted."

"What can you tell us about her?" Micki asked.

"We aren't friends. Barely acquaintances. But when we run into each other, she's friendly enough."

"What did she tell you about the business?" Kat asked.

"Not much, just that it had been a difficult adjustment for her after her husband went missing. She didn't like to talk about her brother-in-law, although she described it more as there not being a lot to say about him because he kept to himself so much. But she gave him credit for being an excellent mortician."

"Did she mention how she felt about her job?" Micki asked.

"Not in so many words. Those times I saw her were business outreach events where she tried to put her best persona on for the funeral home. But I could tell from little things she did or said or didn't say that she wasn't happy."

"Could you describe those things?" Micki pursued.

"I'd ask how things were going, both with the business and with her life, and she'd respond with half answers. And she wouldn't look at me directly. Things like that. I don't remember anything specific."

"Besides describing her brother-in-law as being a loner, how else did she feel about him?" Kat asked.

"She really didn't say. Like I said, she saw her role as being the face of the business, the marketing part. If she and her brother-in-law didn't get along, she wasn't mentioning that."

They weren't getting very far. Hopefully, Marianne and Beau had gotten further when they interviewed Stacia Kerimides. Time to change direction.

"Let's talk a bit about your cohorts on the council," Kat said. "What can you tell us about them?"

Wallace turned wide eyes on her. "Like what? You can learn whatever you need to know about them from their public websites or from your interviews. I assume you're talking to them as well?"

"I'll rephrase my question. What are your impressions of your fellow council members? Are they competent? Can you trust them, both professionally and personally? Do you like them? Things like that."

Wallace drew back in her seat, her right index finger slowly stroking the chair's arm. "I don't see how any of that relates to your investigation."

"Please, Ms. Wallace, just answer the question," Hastings said, surprising Kat that he was still tuned in.

"Right, Deputy. I didn't mean to be impertinent. I don't know any of them very well. In fact, I try not to so as to remain neutral in our deliberations and decision-making. I have the most seniority, which would normally mean I'd be considered the leader. But since I'm the only woman in the group, my seniority occasionally gets overlooked by the men. But for some reason, and not just with this latest issue, the dog park, Busby and McHugh tend to align against Brewster and Sheridan. My power, if you want to call it that, lies in my neutrality and being the swing vote."

"Interesting observation," Micki said. "You said, 'for some reason.' Care to venture a guess why the four men align themselves that way?"

Wallace started to answer then stopped. "It's just something I've observed. We come from diverse occupations, which is what the voters want. I guess you could say Busby, Brewster and I are the creative ones, Busby being a florist, Brewster the architect and me with my art. Dr. McHugh a dentist and Sheridan is the management prof."

Kat couldn't wait until the group reconvened so everyone could compare their impressions of the council members as well as the others they'd interviewed. Avery wasn't giving them much, but maybe that was a clue of its own. At least as far as her involvement, although what had they learned so far about Avery Wallace the woman? It was worth a shot before they ended this interview.

"Perhaps we got ahead of ourselves as we've gotten into this interview," she began. "Other than what you've told us about the other council members and what we can see for ourselves in this gallery, what can you tell us about you?"

Wallace stopped fingering the chair arm and switched to swiveling right, then left and back again. "First thing, I didn't kill Gordon Kerimides. That should be enough to know about me, but to save Deputy Hastings from having to caution me to speak up, I'll go on. I'm forty-four and single. I was married briefly in my twenties, but that didn't work out, although my husband and I parted amicably. I graduated with a fine arts degree from the U of Florida. I worked my way up in a couple galleries, first in Atlanta and then New York City. My goal was always to have my own gallery. I inherited a tidy sum from my grandfather seven years ago with just one condition, that whatever I did with the money, I would do it in Florida. Which is why I'm here.

"I did my due diligence with opportunities in the state, and Serendipity Springs popped up on the top of the list. It has taken a while to establish myself, but I'm getting there. When I'm not here, I'm at home learning Italian." She stopped. "Is that what you wanted?"

"Thank you," Kat replied. She checked out Micki, whose nod indicated she didn't have any more questions. "Do you have any ideas about who might have killed Kerimides?"

"I thought I already covered that question."

Kat persisted. "You said you didn't know the man. You might still have some idea about the murderer."

"I ..."

"Try," Micki added.

Wallace took a minute to think about the question. "Okay, I'll take a stab at it. Even though I don't know anything about the details of his death, including the way he was killed, I'd suggest you take note of those details because the killer might be expressing his or her reason for killing him. If I planned to kill someone, although I never would, I would kill them in a way that was meaningful to me but no one else."

Interesting theory. Kat made a mental note to share it with the rest of the group when they debriefed.

The exterior door sounded. "My client has arrived. We

have to terminate this interview. I hope you got whatever information you came for."

Before departing they got her alibi and headed out to the front part of the gallery and then to the door.

"Ladies, it's been real," Hastings called from behind them.

Both Kat and Micki pivoted to face him. "You've been great, Deputy," Kat said. "Colin."

"Yes, thanks from me, too," Micki added.

"Feel up to an afternoon treat?" Kat asked Micki after Hastings took off.

"Something Greta has cooked up?" Micki asked with enthusiasm.

"Actually, I was thinking more about a stop at our favorite coffee shop."

"I thought we planned to put that off until after we've found our killer?"

"I didn't mean that discussion. I just wanted a few minutes to come down before I face Rick, since I think the group is still planning to gather at my place tonight."

"Did I hear you correctly? You're avoiding your beloved fiancé?"

"Avoid is such a strong word. He'll want a full-fledged debrief before the actual debrief later. I need time to put my thoughts in order. I've already forgotten some of what we heard from Drake Busby. A mug of tea will help restart my brain. And I'm really curious what you thought about Avery Wallace."

"You win. Let's rehash our day."

Micki opted for cream and sugar in her coffee, and Kat had English breakfast tea, even though it was late afternoon.

"What was your impression of Drake Busby?" Micki asked.

"He couldn't provide a viable alibi for Kerimides's time of death. But nothing resembling a strong motive emerged. I can't picture Busby killing the man just because he opposed the dog park. Council members run into any number of issues with people who disagree with them."

"I'd be ready to dismiss him as a suspect except for the reason he gave for deciding to support the dog park, his interest in the woman with the dog. That could be true, but my gut is telling me there's more to it than that."

"Maybe we should've asked for her name," Kat said.

"We can always go back to him a second time, if we think it's important. Right now, we have so many details floating around in our heads, I'm becoming selective about what we retain."

"But let's not forget he admitted he knew Kerimides when they were teens and even toured Europe together in a band."

"So we leave a question mark after Busby's name," Micki said.

"What did you think of Avery Wallace?"

"She's a cool one, but that could be a façade." Micki lifted an eyebrow. "Those clothes and haircut could be a costume to help her sell art."

"Even if it is, that's just smart business," Kat said. "And I sort of understand how she sees her position on the council. Even though she's most senior, she's the only woman. Maintaining neutrality could be her best way of being heard."

"I agree, but I didn't hear anything that suggested she had a motive to kill Kerimides."

Kat finished her tea. "I hope the others are having more

success with their interviews. I don't feel like we accomplished much other than hassle Deputy Hastings."

"I can't believe I'm saying this," Micki said, "but we don't have to always be the ones to solve the case. Eliminating unlikely persons of interest is valuable also."

Kat chuckled. "That sounds more like something I'd say rather than you. But you're right. Hopefully the others have had more productive experiences."

Chapter Fourteen

"Where are Marianne and Beau?" Solomon Ridgedale asked by way of greeting to Guy and Rick when they visited his home at Forestdale Condos.

"We're changing things up," Rick said. "Marianne and Beau are already familiar with your story. Since this is a follow-up, we thought we'd do it with a new set of eyes." He then introduced Guy.

Guy took in what he could see of the man's condo. He couldn't help comparing its airy, open arrangement with Micki's tinier, more crowded home. The guy's lack of furniture and accessories probably accounted for the spaciousness.

Guy and Rick took seats on an oversize sectional while Solomon sat in the only easy chair in the room. Before they started, they were met with a braying howl.

Solomon glanced over his shoulder at what appeared to be the kitchen. "That's what started all this, my dog, Daisy. I stuck her in the kitchen while we talk. She's not used to being cooped up in there."

"We'll try to work around her," Rick said, the firm set of his mouth suggesting otherwise.

"I appreciate you all taking on this investigation," Solomon began. "I thought I'd told you everything, but I can see why a second time through might be necessary."

"I'm glad you feel that way," Guy began, "because it may seem like we're repeating things at times, but we're building on what we already know. Let's start with your whereabouts from ten in the evening to eight the next morning the night Gordon Kerimides was killed."

"I have to give you pretty much the same answer that I gave the sheriff. I was here all of that time except from seven to seven ten, when I took Daisy out. Then I was back in until late morning. But only Daisy can vouch for me. At this point, let me say again that I did not kill the man."

"If not you, who do you think did kill him?" Guy asked.

Solomon raised his open hands. "I have no idea. I hardly knew the man, although it doesn't entirely surprise me that someone did him in. He wasn't an agreeable person."

Guy wasn't finished. "If you had to speculate, who might you guess?"

"I'm less qualified than the sheriff's people or you guys."

"But who?" Guy said.

"Probably anyone at the funeral home. Those who had to work with him day after day. That sister-in-law of his. I heard rumors that she still blames him for her husband's disappearance."

"Just rumors?" Rick asked.

"If you want to dignify public guessing with that term. I have no proof, but you kept pushing."

"You said you barely knew him," Guy continued. "That

suggests you did know him to a certain extent. Could you describe your relationship?"

"I'd never heard of the guy until this dog park thing got under way. I really thought I'd—we'd found a solution with that plot of land owned by the town. Only after that did I learn of his objection. The idea of a bunch of dogs making that much commotion running around a walled-in park to disturb mourners in the funeral home across the road didn't make sense to me. So I was surprised when his objection gained ground with the council, at least a couple members.

"After the vote was tabled at the last council meeting, I thought maybe if the two of us discussed everything involved, we could come to some kind of compromise. I went to see him at the funeral home, and although he agreed to talk to me, there was no changing his mind. He wasn't even willing to hear me out. Told me I was wasting the council and thus the town's time with my petty, personal platform. Then he told me to leave, and if I didn't, he'd call the sheriff."

"You went to see him the day after the council meeting?" Guy asked, trying to put that event in the timeline leading up to Kerimides's death.

"Yes. I wanted to dispel his concerns as soon as possible."

"That would have been two days before he was killed," Guy added.

Solomon thought about it. "Yeah, I guess so."

Rick turned to Guy. "That's why he went to Marianne and Beau, who brought him to me. Being on the opposite side of the dog park issue from the victim, rebuffed by Kerimides when he tried to work out a solution and the timing of Kerimides's death are probably why the sheriff brought him in for questioning and, after that, why Solomon asked us to investigate this case. Though he continues to deny his part in the murder, you can see why he's considered a top suspect."

Guy looked at Solomon. "Given that we know all that already, why are we talking to you again, Solomon?"

Solomon cocked his head, reminding Guy of a parakeet his mother once owned. "That's for you to answer. I've told Marianne, Beau and Rick all I know about this case."

"I'm here because I'm not convinced you have," Rick said. "For our team to investigate, we need all the facts."

Solomon shifted position. "I thought I've been pretty open with you guys. But if there's something I've missed, go ahead. Question away."

Solomon's supposedly open demeanor took Guy back to the days when he'd find himself questioning a witness in a courtroom. Many a time he'd taken great pleasure, perhaps too much for his ego, in turning those opening words upside down. "If you're so concerned about being the sheriff's key suspect, why haven't you engaged a lawyer?"

Solomon glanced at Guy. "I thought I already covered that?"

"With the others. Not me. I'm an attorney. I'm not hustling another client. I know how the criminal justice system works, on the same side as Rick but from a different perspective. My friends are more than happy to help you clear your name, but in the end, they're committed to finding the truth and following through on it, even if that should work against you. An attorney would work directly for you."

"You make a good case. It's hard for me to argue against it. I told Rick and the others that I would get representation if I was formally charged. But I haven't been ready to bring counsel on board any sooner than necessary because of things that happened in my past."

Both Guy and now Rick stared at him.

"Go on," Rick said gently.

Solomon bowed his head and didn't respond at first.

"You do realize we've reached a turning point, don't you?" Rick asked.

"It's not easy to talk about."

"So instead, you're letting six people plus Rick plus me invest our time and effort trying to find the real killer?" Guy asked. "They hardly know you, Solomon, and yet they're putting themselves on the line for you. And this all started with a dog park. Are you even sure a dog park is the answer to your dog's extra energy? Have you checked into others in the area like I have?"

That got Solomon's attention. "You have? Have you got a dog?"

"No. Nor do I plan to get one in the immediate future. But the team figured if a dog park was important enough for someone to get killed because he didn't want one near his business, we'd better make sure."

"I read an article online."

"I assume it was quite supportive of the concept?" Guy asked.

"Yeah."

"Perhaps while my friends and I spend the next several days trying to learn the truth about the murder, if you don't plan to engage an attorney, you might at least learn a little more about existing dog parks," Guy said.

Solomon didn't speak for several beats. Guy wasn't sure if he'd scored with his last point or not. But he wasn't ready to call it a day just yet. He sensed he'd hit a soft spot but wasn't sure what it was.

"My late wife was the love of my life," Solomon said, his volume slightly above a whisper. "I would've done anything for her. I never saw it coming when I was served with divorce papers. Work demands caused me to cancel going on a cruise with her. One we'd been planning and looking forward to for some time. I felt so bad, I urged her to go on her own and not miss it because of me. Little did I know she'd meet someone and begin a months-long secret relationship. The divorce hit like a sledgehammer, especially since her divorce lawyer turned out to be the new man in her life. He was good. Very good. They took my house, and most of our savings went into his bill. They were barely married a year when she was hit with an aggressive form of cancer. She was gone within three months. Everything she'd gained in the divorce settlement went to him."

Rick was the first to speak after Solomon's admission. "Tough break. That what brought you to Serendipity Springs?"

"Yeah," Solomon said.

"And why ..." Guy began. "Divorce attorneys can be real sharks. That's supposedly what builds their reputations. There are professional and ethical considerations that can be pursued, if you think he targeted your wife?"

"I looked into those at the time. But she apparently went into the relationship with her eyes open. The cancer couldn't have been predicted. There was nothing further I could do."

"Let me help find you a top-notch criminal defense attorney. You might not need one. Hopefully not. But you still need someone to advise you while this investigation is proceeding."

"I, uh, thank you, Guy. Guess I've been rather foolish."

"Only in not trusting us with that story," Rick said.

As they left, Guy turned back to Solomon. "I'll get you a name soon."

"And I'll do more research online about dog parks."

"Check with your vet, too," Rick said. "Maybe there's some medication you can get for Daisy that will calm her."

"I'll do that."

Chapter Fifteen

*L*ater that afternoon, Rick showered a tad bit longer than usual and took his time selecting what to wear. He chose a brand-new blue knit golf shirt Kat had recently bought him. He stared into his mirror as he combed his hair. Still had most of it even though the sides were now almost fully gray.

His heart raced and his palms itched. Not the kind of excitement he felt whenever he was around Kat, but the stimulation that used to surge through his body at the start of a new case when he was sheriff. He'd been unsure he'd ever feel so amped again now that he'd opened his own investigation business, but apparently it was still there.

In the next half hour his new team would assemble downstairs to report the findings from their first interviews. He had high hopes for their success. In the past, as individuals they'd helped him solve more than a handful of homicides even though sometimes they seemed to get in his way. This time around they were all in this Kerimides thing together.

Helping Sheriff Brian Quinn investigate their city leaders

was quite a challenge, especially for their first case. He hadn't planned on tackling something so high profile right out of the chute, but he'd learned long ago to deal with whatever came down the pike and go with the flow.

He considered a quick shot of cologne and decided against it. Time to meet the troops.

Marianne was the first to report. "We have a couple potentials, but so far we haven't identified anyone as a key suspect."

"Same here," Syd said for herself and Trip.

"Ditto for Kat and me," Micki said.

Rick wasn't surprised. "I didn't expect to hear anything different, or you would have called immediately," he said, hiding his disappointment that one or two major discoveries hadn't emerged. He went to the white board they'd brought into the living room of Kat's house. "Let's list questions that still remain or other follow-up information you need."

Marianne went first. "The sister-in-law, Stacia Kerimides, readily admitted she hadn't been getting along with her brother-in-law. That appeared to be because he was shutting her out of actually doing the undertaking, even though she's trained for it. She's also the one who found him, although we're not sure if she would have been able to haul his body from the embalming room, where it appears he was killed, to the display room and prop him up against a casket.

"We also talked to the funeral director, Warren Meek, and the custodian, Billy Sampson, who arrived within seconds of her screams when she found the body. Both of them told us the man allowed very few people into the embalming room and the surrounding area. The only exceptions were a guy from Shasta who subbed for him occasionally and the guy who picked up some of the waste. We need to follow up with her on this point. Supposedly he told the custodian he didn't want him exposed to the dangerous chemicals and other materials. So why allow the sub access and not Stacia, who was trained to work with them? Plus, who was it that collected the waste?"

Rick scribbled her comments on the white board while Kat took notes. "Okay, that takes care of the crew at the funeral home. Who drew the five council members?" he asked.

"We interviewed Drake Busby, one of the pro-dog-park members," Kat said. "He knew Kerimides from his school days, since they both grew up in Shasta. In fact, they were in a boy band together following graduation but had no contact in the years after that."

"Supposedly he decided to support the dog park to impress some nameless woman who owns a big dog," Micki added. "He didn't back down, even when we questioned that reason, but we think there's more behind his support he's not admitting to."

"We also asked McHugh that question," Trip said. "We didn't let him off with his first response, 'It was good for the community.' Took a bit, but he finally admitted he'd traded his support of Busby for his support of a variance he wanted for his deck. A lot of quid pro quo going on within the council. Probably doesn't mean much for this case but something to keep in mind if we think one of them is our culprit."

"That takes care of the pro-dog-park members," Rick said. "Who had Tad Brewster?"

"That was Beau and me," Marianne said. "We came away with a couple things. First, an observation: Out of the blue, he referred to the victim as Gordon when we were talking. It seemed a bit too personal, although he'd just told us that he and Dan Sheridan had met with Kerimides at his invitation to hear why he opposed the dog park. He also told us that he found the man to be personable, that he treated himself and Dan with respect and took his time answering their questions. That doesn't sound like the person everyone else has been learning about."

"What about Sheridan?" Rick asked. "Since he met with Kerimides along with Brewster, did he have the same feelings about the guy?"

"I've been waiting to hear what the rest of you learned before Trip and I reported our interview of Dan Sheridan," Syd said. "He apparently came across as a different person to everyone else you talked to except Tad Brewster and Dan Sheridan." She related how Kerimides had cut through the red tape for Sheridan when his mother was killed in a horrible accident. How Sheridan had described Kerimides as a "calming influence" during those days. "That's why he was open to hearing about Kerimides's concerns about the dog park.

"But there's more. When we asked if there was anyone he suspected of murdering the man, after suggesting that was our job, he then asked if we'd spoken with Brewster yet. Not exactly like he was adding that name to our list, but for some reason he thought we should check into Brewster's relationship with the man."

"Sheridan overheard Brewster on a few phone calls," Trip put in. "He couldn't tell for sure if Brewster was talking to Kerimides, but he got the idea it was him from certain references to things like 'services' and 'the departed.' When we pushed to get a better idea of the tone of those calls, he backed away from describing them as 'intimate' but did say they were clearly 'friendly.' He offered to check his council minutes to pinpoint the date, since at least one call took place during a break in a council meeting."

Syd wasn't finished. "He also said Brewster left the room when he noted that Sheridan was listening and later apologized, saying it was a 'nervous client.'"

"Anyway," Trip interrupted, "we asked Deputy Martinez if the sheriff could subpoena Brewster's phone records for that period."

"We already took care of that. Sort of," Marianne said. "In fact, he offered us his phone, and Deputy Hastings took it. But that was to prove Brewster had two business calls during the estimated time of death, which is exactly what Hastings found."

Now Beau entered the phone discussion. "But Brewster did suggest the deputy examine his phone records for the weeks before the death, which Hastings said he'd do."

"Then we can at least find out who Brewster was talking to six months ago or whenever it was, once Sheridan checks his meeting notes," Rick said. "Who does that leave?"

"Avery Wallace, the only woman on the council," Micki replied. "Swears she never met the man, although she did run into Stacia Kerimides from time to time at local meetings. Apparently she handled the marketing end of the business. Wallace didn't want to talk about the other council members, claiming she didn't know much about them personally."

"She told us she saw her 'power' on the council as the neutral vote," Kat said. "I suspect that's why she tabled the dog park discussion. So she could broker her vote with the other four members."

Micki chimed in again. "I was about to dismiss her as a suspect until she said something as we were wrapping the interview. Although she didn't venture any suggestions about suspects when asked, she did say we might want to pay attention to how Kerimides was killed. The murderer might be telling us something with that."

"His being strangled?" Trip asked.

"Or propped against the casket?" Beau added.

"And don't forget the dog collar around his neck," Syd said.

"Doesn't tell us much, does it?" Rick asked. "Each of those three goes off in a different direction. Strangling could mean anything. The killer didn't like bloodshed or didn't want a gun to be heard. Or killed him on the spur of the moment with their hands. And that's just one aspect of the way he was killed."

"And the casket part could be trying to point to those in the funeral home as the most likely suspects," Kat said.

"And finally, the dog collar is obvious," Micki added. "Although I don't think that detail has been released to anyone outside our circle."

"One more item we can check off our list for now, Kerimides's condo," Rick said. "Quinn and I have already gone through it. We didn't find anything of interest. In fact, we hardly found anything. The man apparently was a neatness freak. Looked like he spent little time there."

Rick stepped away from the white board. He'd take another look at it later after the others left, hoping to be inspired with a fresh glance. He summoned his enthusiasm to charge up the team. "Congratulations, everyone. Not bad for a first day of your investigation. We've got some specific points to check out tomorrow."

"Before we plan tomorrow, I have a question," Marianne said. "Beau and I worked with both Deputy Martinez and Deputy Hastings today. Neither seemed particularly pleased with their assignments. Should we anticipate that reaction with future cases?"

"Did they impede your investigation?" Rick asked.

"No, not at all," she replied. "They were polite and let us do our thing once they introduced us to the people we interviewed. But they each made a point of meeting with us just prior to the interview to go over the game plan. You've told us more than once how much you appreciated them when they worked for you. So we tried to abide by their rules. Do they feel like we're taking their jobs?"

Rick rubbed the back of his neck. "Did the rest of you sense some hesitation on their part?"

All the others nodded. "Kat and I received a mini lecture from Deputy Hastings before our first interview. He reiterated his stance but less so as we began the second interview," Micki said.

"I didn't get the sense that they feared for their jobs," Kat replied. "They are both competent and confident people. But they and the rest of the sheriff's staff have been through a difficult year. It seemed to me that Colin was feeling his way through what must seem like another new challenge. He seemed to have mellowed somewhat by the end of our second interview."

"I agree," Syd added, "although I got the impression they were hoping their obligation would only extend to today."

"Thanks for those reactions," Rick told the group. He'd been concerned that Martinez and Hastings might feel slighted having to work with the team, but he also knew they were professionals. They would handle this investigation with their usual dedication to the job. "We need to keep two things in mind. First, today was a first for all of us. You women have investigated in the past but never this, uh, formally. You guys have done your part as well. But this time you are part of an official team, an officially backed team. And second, this is a unique situation. Sheriff Quinn is still feeling his way as sheriff and knows he's walking on eggshells with so many members of the council potentially involved. Our team presented a unique opportunity. This arrangement is something I should discuss with Brian. But let's give it another day to assess how big a problem his people have working with us."

He returned his attention to his jottings on the white board. "It would appear that no one person emerged as a likely suspect after your interviews. Is that a correct assumption?"

The other seven exchanged looks. "More or less," Marianne said, acting as spokesperson. "So far, from what we heard tonight, Stacia Kerimides appears to have the strongest reasons for wanting him out of her life. But were those strong enough to kill him? It's hard to say."

"Including why he was so adamant about not letting anyone into the embalming area," Beau added. "Other than the sub and the guy or the company that disposed of some of the waste. We need to know more about that."

"So, more follow-up with Stacia Kerimides," Rick said, summarizing for Marianne and Beau.

Syd now spoke. "We need to check back with Councilman Sheridan and pin him down on the dates when he overheard Brewster on the phone with someone who could have been Kerimides, long before they met with him."

"Until we know those dates, we shouldn't approach Brewster," Beau said. "And then, only if we get access to his phone records."

"I wouldn't dismiss either the custodian or the funeral services director," Marianne added, "since they were both in the building, or in Meek's case arrived a little later, the morning Kerimides's body was found. The custodian, Billy Sampson, admitted Kerimides had threatened to fire him if he ever went to the embalming area again. Maybe that was too great a temptation, and when he did go in there, he found something, something he was using to blackmail the guy."

"Wow. That's going a little overboard on speculation, don't you think?" Guy asked.

"Maybe," she replied. "But I can't get past the fact that the embalming area was off-limits to almost everyone, and therefore it held special importance to Gordon Kerimides. Why? And even though his body was found in the display room, there's evidence some kind of scuffle happened in the embalming room. Again, why?"

"Those are very good questions, Marianne," Rick told her.

"Although we checked out the display room, where the body was found, we put off seeing the embalming room just yet," she said.

"Why?" Micki asked. "You just said you thought it was critical to the case."

"That's right," Marianne replied. She turned to Rick. "I couldn't do it today. Sorry. We were halfway through our interview with Stacia Kerimides when my cousin's funeral last year came back to me."

"Jeanie?" Beau asked. "You didn't mention that to me, either before going in or afterwards."

"I thought I'd put it behind me. We weren't all that close in later years, but we grew up together back in Pennsylvania, and the more Stacia talked, the more that funeral came screaming back to me. I thought I could handle the display room, but I wasn't up to seeing the embalming room today. But I'll get my act together tonight, and I'll be ready to tour it tomorrow."

"She's shielding me," Beau said. "Jeanie was my cousin. I'm the one who thought I could get through all the funeral home stuff, but Marianne caught one look at me and decided the embalming room was too much."

"I'll go with Marianne tomorrow, if you'd prefer not to," Micki told Beau. "I'm curious to see one."

"Okay, hold up a minute, everyone," Rick said, sensing it was time to take control again. He hadn't planned to shake up the partnerships so soon, feeling continuity was important in their early days as a team. But Beau's hesitation to tour the embalming room forced the question. These were all capable people. Each brought his or her own strengths to the table, so why not give a new alignment a try?

"Beau, if you don't mind, tomorrow Micki will accompany Marianne to interview Stacia Kerimides a second time and check out the embalming room. It makes sense to send a fresh set of eyes with Marianne," he said. "Kat, instead of teaming up with Micki, you work with Guy on the transcripts of Brewster and Kerimides's phone calls. Once we get his name from Stacia Kerimides, Beau and Trip, how about taking a short trip over to Shasta to interview the substitute mortician? Does everyone have a job?'

"Not me," Syd said. "Do you want to interview any of the council members again?"

"Let's wait until we've been through the phone, email and text transcripts. Why don't you join Kat and Guy going through those? Three sets of eyes can plow through them quicker." How had he forgotten Syd? He made a mental note to include her in whatever follow-up activities emerged from this newest set of assignments.

As soon as the group dispersed, Rick holed up in his study with a phone call to Sheriff Brian Quinn. Though the subject of subpoenaing various phones had come up during the meeting, Kat was pretty sure he wanted to ask about the two deputies as well.

He was gone over thirty minutes. When he emerged, Kat had a cup of herbal tea and two cookies ready for him just in case the call had gone south.

"What did he tell you about Martinez and Hastings?" she asked.

"It was like a game of tag. First he protected his people, glossing over any objections they might have voiced about working with our team, and then I hedged on how much longer we'd be interviewing persons of interest and potential suspects, since no one so far has risen to the top of our list. He did agree to subpoena Brewster's phone, and he already has someone looking into the finances of the funeral home. I decided it was too soon to ask how he thought this arrangement between his office and our team was working."

She set down her own cup of tea. "Is it too soon for me to ask you the same question?"

"Like I told the others, you may all have investigated murders in the past but not in the same quasi-official capacity as you are now. That's a huge adjustment. Add to that the fact we're all just feeling our way as a team. I'd say we did pretty well for a first day. That's huge. With so many people involved, a lot could have gone wrong, blown up in our faces. But that didn't happen. In fact, Brian did say that both Pilar and Colin were impressed with the way you all handled yourselves and the questions you asked."

She sat up with that news. "That's huge! We can't ask for a better endorsement at this point."

He snaked an arm around her shoulders. "You're right. It hasn't been obvious, but I've been wound up all day, anxious to see this team approach work. I didn't realize transitioning from being sheriff in charge of a group of people would be so ... different."

Not obvious? Perhaps not to the others, but she'd been aware of his tension. She fought to subvert the relief surging through her with his admission. Sharing his concerns was a positive step toward dealing with them. Moreover, it was one more sign that marrying him was the best decision she'd ever made. "What can I do to help?"

He returned an affectionate squeeze. "You already have just by listening to me." He lifted his cup with his free hand. "And by thoughtful things like this."

"I'm glad you're feeling good about our progress. The only other thing I have to say is, let Day Two begin!"

Chapter Sixteen

"At least one of us can sleep," Beau said when he walked into the kitchen at nine fifteen later that evening and noted Mortimer conked out in his doggie bed in a corner of the room.

"He's been fed and watered and taken outside one last time today," Marianne replied.

"You're baking cookies," Beau said. "Someone who didn't know you might wonder why you've decided to pursue this endeavor so close to our bedtime. But now that I've almost attained my PI intern license, I know that means you're thinking about the meeting we just left. Processing. Working through one or two angles you can't quite let go."

"This has nothing to do with your prowess as a fledgling detective," Marianne replied, offering him a spoonful of dough. "You know me too well. But you're right about what got me baking at this hour. Like I said to our team, I can't help thinking we were so close to discovering the murderer or at least the motive when we were at the funeral home. But we missed it." She put down the wooden spoon she'd been using to finish blending the ingredients and stared directly at him.

"How did that happen, Beau? We may still be viewed as amateurs, but we've been sleuthing long enough to have picked up on anything unusual."

"It was our first time there and our first swipe at the case. And there was so much to see and hear."

"That's the crux of the matter. So much. We were bombarded from every direction to the point where details that didn't matter got mixed up with major clues."

"I'm sorry I let being in the funeral home get to me. I really thought I could handle it," he said.

"It's okay, Beau. You tried."

"With your pharmaceutical background, you'll do great in the embalming room. I'm glad Micki wanted to step up and take my place."

"But now you're going to another funeral home when you and Trip interview the sub over in Shasta."

"As long as I don't have to see the actual room where the dead are handled, I should be okay."

"I hope Stacia is up to accompanying us. She may not have been allowed access in the past, but she still has the expertise. She'll know what should be there, and if there's anything out of order, she should be able to find it."

"If she's willing to go in there," Beau said.

"I suppose that's possible, but I bet she's been waiting to see what he's been hiding from everyone all this time. She may even be considering taking over his duties. Would you mind watching these cookies while they bake? I want to go online and research embalming rooms."

Beau picked up the baking tray filled with drops of cookie dough and shoved it into the oven. Miraculously, Mortimer slept on. "How long do I set the timer for?"

"Eleven minutes. Thanks. I won't stay up long. Just long enough to get a feel for the essentials."

He stared her down, his forehead lined with wrinkles. "Don't go overboard, okay? I don't want you having nightmares. You need your sleep before you tackle Day Two."

"Don't worry about me," she called over her shoulder as she left the room. She pivoted and returned. "Don't you go overboard either with those cookies. I don't want you up all night with a stomachache."

"Touché," he called after her disappearing back.

"ARE you sure you want to check out that embalming area?" Guy asked Micki once they had returned to her condo.

"Yes. Why do you ask?" she replied. "It's not like there'll be a dead body we have to work around."

"No, since all the local deaths have been rerouted to Shasta for the time being. But your imagination, that wonderful part of your brain that accounts for your articles, might do you in if you start imagining how all the chemicals and instruments you find there are used."

"Thanks for planting that idea in my mind. The possibility hadn't occurred to me until now."

"Sorry. Maybe I'm just envious. I'd like to check it out myself."

"Rick gave me copies of the crime scene photos taken by the forensics team if you want to see them. I just glanced at them long enough to familiarize myself with the layout."

"What did they tell you?" he asked.

"It's clear some kind of fight or brawl took place there due to what appeared to be a large pool of dried blood on the floor. We're assuming it belonged to Kerimides because of the head trauma he suffered. Plus, there are objects strewn about the room. But he must have been knocked out or even killed before it got too serious, or more of the chemicals and other goodies in the room would have been broken and spilled."

"Interesting insights. You probably wouldn't need to actually see the room with those in mind."

"True, but the journalist in me wants to view it firsthand."

"And you couldn't let Marianne upstage you," he added. Sweetly.

"That would never happen."

"Got it. How dare I even suggest such a thing?"

Chapter Seventeen

"I thought I covered everything with the couple that interviewed me yesterday," Stacia Kerimides said to Deputy Martinez, Marianne and Micki.

"Mrs. Putnam and Ms. Demetrius are here to follow up on information obtained after your interview yesterday," Martinez told her.

"I'm back for continuity's sake, but Ms. Demetrius is here with a new set of eyes and ears," Marianne said.

Stacia emitted a heavy sigh. "I suppose it's necessary in order to discover who killed Gordon and also so we can open our doors again. What do you want to know?"

"We heard not only from you but also the custodian and the funeral director that your brother-in-law jealously guarded the embalming area, allowing in only the occasional substitute and someone who collects some of the waste," Marianne began. "Could you tell us more about that?"

"I don't know what more there is to say. Gordon only cared about the undertaking part of running a funeral home. The only administrative part he was interested in was the expenses associated with preparing the bodies, and he didn't participate at all in the services. When my husband, Tom, was alive, I occasionally helped out in the embalming area. But since his disappearance, Gordon wouldn't let me anywhere near the area."

Micki spoke for the first time. "But he gave no explanation for keeping you away?"

"I tried to pin him down on that more than once, but all he'd say was that he was the expert and the only way to maintain that distinction for our business was for him to be the sole person who worked there. His explanation didn't ring true, but it's been easier for me to defer to his claim than to fight him on it. At times I've suspected it wasn't so much how good he was at preparing bodies as it was he didn't have the confidence to handle the rest of operations."

"Who served as his substitute?"

"John Seymour in Shasta. He works at the funeral home there most of the time, along with two others. They're handling the deaths around here until we can resume our business."

"What about the other guy?" Micki asked. "Who picked up the waste?"

"I don't know much about that. The lab is set up to get rid of certain waste through our own disposal system. But some human waste doesn't lend itself to that system and must be picked up by a company devoted to that type of hazardous waste. I can get you the company's name, but they'll have to tell you who regularly serviced us."

"We'd like that name now," Micki pursued.

Stacia keyed in a prompt on her computer. "Torrance Waste Removal." She gave them a phone number and address.

"Do you know anything about that process?" Beau asked.

"Not much, not even what days they pick up. Whatever waste there is to be disposed of is taken away from the back entrance that leads directly to the embalming room. It is unlocked during the day, but it's the custodian's duty to lock it each night."

"What do you know about your brother-in-law staying through the night at times?" Micki asked.

Stacia blinked once. "Nothing. There were mornings when I suspected that might have been the case, but Gordon and I never discussed it. I suppose it's possible, especially if a body needed extra attention. There's room by that entrance I mentioned for him to have parked his SUV out back."

"Has anything else occurred to you since we spoke yesterday?" Marianne asked.

Instead of answering her question, Stacia rose and swiveled to stare out the window behind her desk. She remained there for several seconds.

"Mrs. Kerimides?" Martinez finally asked. "Has something occurred to you?"

Stacia turned slowly. "I'm not sure. I'm debating whether this is meaningful or not."

"Why not let us decide that?" Micki said in an encouraging tone.

Stacia took her seat again. "A couple weeks ago, he came to this office, shut the door and asked—asked, mind you—for a few minutes of my time. He wanted to know if I was aware of the great dog park issue before the town council. I told him that I'd heard a little about it at a meeting I'd attended at the women's club, but since I didn't have a dog of my own, I hadn't paid much attention.

"He went on to say he was totally opposed to the idea because it would be located on the empty lot behind the funeral home. Gordon rarely paid attention to anything happening in the outside world unless it involved the potential deaths of citizens. When I asked why, he gave me this look that suggested he couldn't believe I could be so obtuse and said, 'the noise, of course.' I asked how noise could possibly affect his work, since the embalming area is virtually soundproof. He proceeded to point out how much the sound of barking dogs, the noise, would disturb our mourners.

"I asked how he even knew that since he was a stranger to our services, which he sloughed off. But then he asked me to be just as concerned in case anyone asked my opinion on the noise issue."

"Okay?" Micki asked. "Why are you bringing this up?"

"Gordon never asked me to do anything. He always demanded. He really did not want the dog park to go in behind us."

"You're saying your brother-in-law wasn't concerned about the noise even though he was still very much against the dog park?" Marianne asked.

"That is the way it seems. Is that helpful?"

"It may be," Micki replied. "Does that mean you would have no objections to a dog park now?"

"Not until I find out why Gordon didn't want it. I hope your investigation will uncover that."

"We'll take that under consideration," Marianne said.

When it appeared that neither Micki nor Marianne had further questions, Martinez took charge. "The next step in our investigation is a tour of the embalming area, since our forensics people have finished their initial review. It would help if you participated, since you are familiar with the process, even if you haven't been there for some time."

Stacia covered her heart with a hand. "You want me to go in there?"

"It's your property, Mrs. Kerimides," Martinez said. "But if you prefer, we'll find another expert. Perhaps the undertaker from Shasta, John Seymour, could help?"

Stacia thought about it. "No, that won't be necessary. I need to take charge sometime. I might as well start now."

WHILE STACIA WENT to change from her business suit to more informal clothes, Deputy Martinez quizzed Marianne and Micki. "Are you both prepared for this?" she asked. "Of course there will be no bodies there, but someone with a vivid imagination might find this tour overwhelming. I've not seen this room, but in my early days as a deputy I was exposed to the one over in Shasta. I almost had to leave the room, so just give me a high sign if it gets to be too much."

"Marianne is the creative one with her one-act plays and all. I'm the journalist. I go by the facts," Micki replied.

Marianne shot a questionable look toward Micki. Was she deliberately setting her up for a negative reaction to the experience?

"Okay, I just wanted to prepare you," Martinez said. "Mrs. Kerimides should be back momentarily once she's changed clothes."

"Billy Sampson, our custodian, will meet us at the door. I haven't claimed the keys to the room yet," Stacia told them after she returned and locked her office. "This is my first time seeing the area since the incident. In fact, I haven't been there very often over the years, as I mentioned yesterday in my interview."

"We appreciate your taking the time to do this," Marianne said.

Stacia pointed out various parts of the home as they made their way: a couple of private counseling rooms near her office; the service area; the private room next door for the family to use until the service began; a small reception area, where mourners gathered before admission to the service; the larger reception area for gathering and coffee post-service; the exit where the caskets were loaded onto waiting hearses; and finally, the display area. Near the back, they took a large elevator to a lower part of the building.

"This elevator is not available to the public," Stacia said. "It is large enough to move the casket from the display area down to the embalming area, where the body is placed in it, and then back up to this level again and to the family room for private viewing before the service."

Marianne let her mind picture a casket riding along with them. She'd never paid much attention to all that went on in a funeral home. Over the years, when she'd attended services or viewings, she'd been content to let the business behind death and post-death activities remain mysteries. Now, the whole process was being drawn into sharp focus. Why had Micki planted the idea of her overreacting to this tour in her brain? She had every confidence she would be fine, but she didn't need Micki's suggestion.

"That back entrance straight ahead is where bodies and other deliveries are received," Stacia said when the elevator door opened. "The embalming suite is to the left, and the custodian's area and other storage are located on the right."

Billy Sampson was waiting for them at the first door on the corridor to the left. "I opened the room but didn't go in," he told Stacia.

"Thanks, Billy. I'll let you know when you can close up again," she said, dismissing him.

Apparently she didn't want the keys just yet.

"I'll go in first and turn on the lights," Stacia said. "Be prepared. The overhead lighting will be bright."

Thirty seconds later, Marianne and Micki went into the room together. Even though they'd been warned about the brightness, the first thing Marianne noticed was the smell. Something akin to the distasteful odor of disinfectant she knew from hospitals.

Stacia sniffed the air. "I'd forgotten about the heavy perfume that never seems to dissipate. It's from formaldehyde and other solutions used to cover the smell of human waste. Give it a minute or two. It won't go away, but you'll get somewhat used to it." She worked some controls on the wall just inside the door. "I turned on the air filtration system. It usually runs all the time, but the forensic people must have turned it off when they finished."

The lighting gave the room a surreal quality. As her eyes adjusted to the brightness, Marianne noticed the large table in the middle of the room. On casters, it appeared to have been knocked off its usual position. A narrow channel ran around the stainless-steel tabletop about two inches from the perimeter, with an opening on one side for the disposal of fluids. A container of some sort was attached underneath. She didn't want to contemplate its operation much further.

A dark stain, roughly three feet long and eighteen inches wide, covered the floor to the side of the examining table. The forensic photos they'd viewed earlier had caught it when it was still wet.

Counters formed an *L* around two of the walls. Above one, two shelves held numerous containers and bottles. A cabinet occupied half of the other wall. One door was open, and several open boxes spilled their contents onto the floor. Another wide door and counter with cabinets ran along the third wall.

"I can describe what you're seeing, if you want that much information," Stacia said.

Micki was ready. "There's just one table. What if there was more than one body?"

"Good question. Some morticians prefer a larger room to accommodate more than one body at a time, but early on, Tom and Gordon decided they just wanted to focus on one person at a time. They cut the room in half. That door over on the other wall takes you into the waiting room. It's not as cold as most morgues, but the temp is low enough to preserve the occupants."

"Before we go there, could you name some of the items on the shelves and in the cabinet?" Marianne asked.

Stacia switched her gaze to the two shelves along the one wall, her eyes narrowing. "Is that necessary?"

"No, I guess not, if that's a problem," Marianne replied. "I thought it might give us a better feel for your brother-in-law's everyday surroundings."

Their tour guide made her way slowly toward the shelves and studied the contents. "These are mostly the chemicals used to embalm the body: solutions made mostly of formaldehyde, fluids that are injected into the torso organs, dyes and humectants." Her tone had gone flat, as if being so close to the items she had not seen in years was a strain. "Although the process is much more complicated, it mainly involves opening up the body cavity, draining it, and injecting into it a combination of these solutions to initiate deterioration of the body once buried."

Perhaps a tad more information than Marianne anticipated, but then, she had asked for details. She wasn't sure if Stacia's remarks were meant to be helpful or "in your face," since Marianne had pushed for it. The wealth of details did nothing to quash her fascination.

Stacia pulled out a drawer under the counter. "You want to know how they're injected? These are some of the tools: various types of aspirators, arterial tubes and cannulas, scalpels." She reached in a jacket pocket and put on a pair of disposable gloves. Then she picked up a long needle attached to a hose. "This is a trocar. It is used to suction fluids."

"Mrrrph."

Marianne had been so focused on Stacia's comments, she hadn't noticed Micki behind her. Now she turned to find her investigation partner had doubled up. "Micki?" She took two long steps back to her friend just as Martinez caught her.

"I think this tour has gotten too real for her," Martinez told Marianne.

"I-I'm fine," Micki managed to get out. "Just a little woozy."

"There's a room two doors down that Gordon used as an office," Stacia called. "There should still be bottled water in the fridge."

Martinez guided Micki out the door.

"That's why I asked if you really wanted me to describe the room's contents," Stacia said. "That sometimes happened back when I was allowed in this room and led tours."

"My partner will be so embarrassed she reacted like that."

"How about you? Are you okay?"

"Yes. This is all very interesting, although I think I've gotten the gist of how it happens. But it surprises me he performed the whole process by himself," Marianne replied.

"Many morticians have assistants, but not Gordon. He preferred to do everything on his own. Even facial reconstruction when necessary and the makeup. All that equipment, prosthetics and cosmetics are over there on the third wall.

"It helped that he was a big man. When he was younger, so Tom told me, he built up his body enough to do all the heavy lifting on his own." She closed the drawer holding the instruments but continued staring at the shelves.

"Is something out of order?" Marianne asked.

"Perhaps. This is ... unexpected. Unless Gordon changed his approach in recent years, there appear to more solutions here than would be typical."

"Maybe he was ordering ahead?"

"Possibly, but there are some items here I wouldn't expect to see. They are also solutions but not typically used for embalming. At least not a human body."

"Like what?"

"Sodium hydroxide for one. And distilled water." She offered Marianne a baffled look.

"Anomalies like that are the kinds of things we wanted to know."

"Are we finished here?" Stacia asked coldly.

"Yes, let's see how Ms. Demetrius is doing," Marianne said, pivoting to leave.

"Wait," Stacia called from behind her. "I just noticed these waste containers stacked over here by the cabinet. There are four. Typically, I'd expect to find two. Some have red lettering on them. The lettering on the others is black."

"Is that important?"

"It could be. Red labels usually refer to biohazardous waste. Why are two of them black? It's my understanding they're only picked up once a week. There are enough here for twice our usual population."

"I'll make note of your observations," Marianne said.

Micki's complexion was almost back to its normal color when they walked into the room Stacia had said served as her brother-in-law's office. Micki was lying on a day bed, but she sat up when she saw them. "Mrs. Kerimides, I'm so sorry I wonked out on you," she said immediately. "I'm a journalist. I've witnessed all ranges of human tragedy. That's never happened to me when I've covered other stories."

"Don't worry about it. Mrs. Putnam appears to have seen what she needed to see. I'll wait here with you until you feel ready to go upstairs again, but I do need to get back to my regular job."

"Of course," Marianne said.

"Just give me a few minutes," Micki said. "I'm almost back to normal."

Chapter Eighteen

Ten minutes later, the pair had thanked Stacia Kerimides and were heading to Marianne's car.

"One more time, are you sure you're okay?" Martinez asked. "I can't leave you until I know you're fine."

"I truly am okay, Deputy. I'm sorry to have put you in this position. You have to ensure your department is not liable for whatever happened to me. If I need to sign something, I will."

"I'll get back to you on that. I believe you, but I have to think of the department, especially since the way this investigation is being handled is an experiment."

"Go ahead and say it," Micki said once just she and Marianne were back in Marianne's car. "There I was, concerned about you having a bad reaction to that room, and then I went and succumbed to it."

"Truth be told, for a nanosecond I thought it ironic, but mainly I was worried about you. Are you okay now?"

"Other than being embarrassed, I'm back. What did I miss? I zoned out as soon as she brought up the process of draining the body."

"Let me think. A couple things surprised Stacia. I was so

busy worrying about you, I didn't process what she said fully. She took a closer look at the items on the shelves on that far wall and commented that there was more of something than she would've expected and there was something else she wouldn't have expected."

"That could be important. Take a minute to rerun her words in your brain."

"Actually, I jotted down a few notes. Go ahead and remove the notepad from my purse, since I'm driving."

Micki did as suggested and flipped to the page of notes. "It says, 'too much some solutions? why NaOH and distilled water?' I know Na is sodium; O is oxygen; is H hydrogen?"

"Yes. Together it's sodium hydroxide, better known in some forms as sodium lye. If I recall my chemistry, it's used to adjust pH in some commercial products. The distilled water might be used to dissolve something."

"Translate that to their presence in an embalming room," Micki said.

"That's just it. Stacia, the expert, couldn't, although she's been away from the actual process for years."

Micki stared at Marianne's notes a minute. "For all that room holds, it wasn't that big. Why would Kerimides take up precious space for those items?"

"That's one question we have to pursue. There's more. Look at that second note."

"Waste containers different color lettering," Micki read. "What difference would the colors make?"

"Possibly everything when you're working with biohazardous materials. At least it was enough to throw Stacia. She couldn't explain it. Nor could she explain why there were more containers than she would've thought necessary."

"Let me get this straight without going faint again. Are these containers what are used to dispose of body stuff that is too hazardous to go down that drain on the side of the table?"

"Take a breath and look straight ahead. Yes," Marianne answered, sneaking a glimpse at her friend to make sure she was okay.

Micki did as suggested and didn't speak for several beats while she took large breaths. "I'm just an outsider, but here's my guess. If there were too many, some of them, the ones with whatever color lettering wasn't the norm, were being used for something else."

"My conclusion exactly."

"And there being too much of some of the solutions and some there that shouldn't be there—" Micki went on. "Perhaps whatever they were intended for involved the extra containers?"

"We just need to figure out what that other purpose was," Marianne said. "That could be a number of things: industrial purposes, explosives, drugs to name a few."

"We already have been told by more than one person interviewed that Kerimides was a private person. Maybe that was a cover, a reason for keeping anyone else from finding out what he was up to," Micki said.

"Add to that the fact that only he and the custodian had keys to that part of the building," Marianne said.

"And the embalming area was just down the hall from a back entrance," Micki added.

"A private entrance that was unlocked during the day and locked every evening."

"Meaning that if Kerimides was dealing in things other than just the disposal of biohazardous waste, that back entrance could have been used for traffic no one had any inkling about."

Marianne exchanged looks with Micki while they waited for a stoplight to change. "We need to share these thoughts with the others right away," Marianne said. "Although what she saw surprised her, we don't know what Stacia will do with that information."

"All this makes what I discovered in his so-called office all the more interesting," Micki said. "You saw the day bed I lay down on. There was also a television, a refrigerator, a hot plate and a closet where I'm guessing he kept part of his wardrobe. In other words, that room was serving as his home away from home. Whatever he was up to besides preparing bodies could have been done twenty-four hours a day with no one the wiser."

"Everything we've learned still begs the question, why?" Marianne said.

"Money?"

"Most likely, but why, simply out of greed, since this business seems to have been doing pretty well? Or for some other reason?"

"Quinn's forensic people have to dig deeper into Kerimides's financial records."

"Kat, Syd and Guy are going through the transcripts of both his phone and Brewster's," Marianne said. "Maybe there's a clue there who he was dealing with, because those containers were going somewhere. I doubt he would've left the premises with them."

They drove another few blocks until Marianne pulled the car over to the curb.

"Why are we stopping?" Micki asked.

"I don't know about you, but I'm super stoked. I've got more energy than I know what to do with."

"Too much just to get a coffee?" Micki asked.

"Maybe later. Want to go for a run?"

"Since when have you gone running?"

"Beats me. It just seemed like the best way to get rid of all this juice running through my veins."

"Do you even have running shoes? Or a jogging outfit?"

"Do you?" Marianne asked.

"As a matter of fact, I'm fully outfitted thanks to a bee Guy got in his bonnet a few months ago. Thought we could enjoy more time together if we jogged together every day. Nice idea. Lasted about a week. No, five days. If you're serious, we could swing by my place and I'll change."

Marianne had to laugh. "I didn't realize Guy was such an optimist. It'd be worth it just to see you all duded up, but now that I've thought about this idea a bit, let's just walk around the lake downtown. I still need to expend some energy, emphasis on some, but there's too much involved with getting ready to run."

"Walking it is," Micki replied.

Marianne pulled away from the curb and turned right at the next cross street. Five minutes later, they parked in front of their favorite coffee shop, the one next to the lake, and headed to the walking path.

"Should we be doing some stretching exercises first?" Micki asked.

Marianne checked the surrounding area for others. One woman was jogging about two hundred feet ahead of them. Two joggers were coming in from their sprint around the lake. "Okay, show me what to do."

Micki spread her feet and extended her arms to the side. "First, you just bend to the right and then the left. Do that five times."

The two of them tried that move in tandem.

"Now, bend over and touch your toes. Five times for this, too."

It looked so easy when Micki did it, but each move was a challenge for Marianne. "Are we done yet?" she asked.

"Not really, but we'll stop, since you appear to be in pain. Do you think you can make it all around the lake?"

Making a full circuit was looking less likely, but since this had been her idea, Marianne was determined to give it a shot.

They took their time, not speaking at first. Fortunately, Marianne had discovered an old pair of sneakers in her car's trunk, so even though she was still wearing her slacks and knit top, she was comfortable.

They entered the wooded part of the trail. The lake stayed with them on one side, the sun sparkling off the surface, but the other side provided welcome shade, since the temp was now in the mid-eighties.

"How're you doing?" Micki asked at the halfway point.

Whether they gave up and retraced their path or finished the trail, it would be the same distance. "I'm fine," Marianne lied. "I should do this more often. I might actually lose some weight. Better than taking one of those weight-loss drugs."

"The stuff you inject once a week? I considered taking one a while back but dropped the idea before it got very far. I couldn't imagine self-injecting. Plus, they're quite expensive."

Micki stared at her a few beats.

"What?" Marianne asked.

"That look on your face scared me. I wonder if it's what

Guy sees when some crazy notion about a story occurs to me."

"Don't panic. Just a fleeting thought. I need to do more research first," Marianne said, attempting to reassure her friend she hadn't lost her marbles.

After they'd gone another hundred feet, Micki pulled up.

"I'm okay, really. We don't have to keep stopping to rest," Marianne said as she took several deep breaths.

"I thought stopping here would be appropriate as we tackle our first case as a real team," Micki replied. "Remember this place?"

They'd reached an opening that led to a wood plank overlook, beyond which the ground gave way to a shallow swamp.

"This is where the battered body of Paul Schwimmer was found, which led our fellow mah jongg player Olivia to seek out Syd's help finding the real killer before she was arrested."

"And overwhelmed with the task, Syd enlisted you, me and Kat to help her find the culprit," Micki said.

Marianne shook her head. "That seems so long ago, but it was just a few years back."

"We've come a long way, pal. I think that buzz you've been feeling is your brain telling you we've almost got this one."

Marianne considered her friend's assessment of her mood. "You're right! But my brain is also asking me where we go from here."

"First, we finish this walk. Then we lay our theory on the rest of the team and hope some of them have filled in a few more blanks."

Chapter Nineteen

"I'm just about to drop off to sleep," Guy told Kat and Syd. "How about you guys?"

It was early afternoon. The three were seated around the table in Kat's kitchen, the transcripts from both phones spread out before them. Since Brewster's pile of phone, text and email messages was double the size of Kerimides's, Kat and Syd divided it up while Guy went through Kerimides's pile.

The plan was to trade once they each finished their first set.

"Where's Greta today? Syd asked.

"I bribed her with a gift card to her favorite restaurant downtown so she wouldn't think she had to keep feeding us while we work," Kat said.

"Too bad," Syd replied. "I always enjoy her making a fuss over me when I'm here."

"Not to worry. The coffeepot is full, and the fridge is filled with sandwich makings and dips, plus there's chips and cookies on the counter. I didn't want her hovering while we worked. Not that she would give away anything we're reviewing, but she'd want to help."

"Liability concerns?" Guy asked.

"Exactly. That's more to placate Rick. I have to respect his concerns as he's setting up this new business."

"If she doesn't return before we leave, thank her for all the goodies," Guy said.

After several more minutes, they took a brief break and began to hit the treats Greta had left for them.

"How far have you each gotten?" Kat asked the other two before they resumed their review.

"Kerimides appears to have done his business either on the phone or by text," Guy said. "There are few emails. The phone calls were mostly to businesses dealing with the embalming part of the business. Very few of what appear to be private calls. Texts were mainly to the custodian and the substitute mortician. On occasion, he called his sister-in-law. Those calls lasted under two minutes."

"Tad Brewster made and received a lot of phone calls," Kat said. "I did a quick pass on everything to gauge how much is here, and then I started a call-by-call review. Despite having what appears to be a thriving architectural business, he seems to spend a considerable amount of his time on the phone. Probably growing his clientele. How about you, Syd? Are you getting a different perspective as you go through his emails and texts?"

"I'm only through the first eight months," Syd said. "Nothing major to report."

Guy rubbed the back of his neck. "I didn't plan on this project taking so much time or being so boring."

"Didn't you spend hours reading contracts and the like

before you retired?" Syd asked. "This isn't so much different, other than probably easier because there's less legalese to decipher."

"Legalese I understand, but this stuff is like eavesdropping on someone's personal and public life. Especially when thus far nothing is jumping out as related to this case."

An hour later, they once again checked in with each other. Guy had finished Kerimides's transcripts. Syd was almost done with Brewster's emails, having already finished the texts. Kat was almost finished with the phone calls.

"I'm trying not to be discouraged that we've discovered so little," Guy said. "At least the team can now check off the communications of these two key players in this case."

Syd didn't reply at first. "Did it strike you as odd that we didn't find any of the calls Dan Sheridan thought had transpired between these two guys?"

Guy thumped his forehead. "I got so involved looking for things that stood out, I forgot about what Sheridan had told us. Does the fact we didn't find anything mean he was in error?"

"Perhaps. But he seemed so sure when Trip and I talked to him," Syd said. "Not about what he overheard exactly but the fact that he did witness Brewster on a few private calls."

"Guess that gives us something to report to the team."

"I'm not ready to give up just yet. One of our PI trainers told us never to trust evidence one hundred percent when it runs counter to that of a personal witness. That sounds heretical to our task as detectives, because human memory can be faulty, but right now it's got me wondering if we've missed something in our review," Syd said.

"You're talking to the man who has lived by the facts all

his career, Syd. Convince me there's more to what we've found."

"That's a tall order, making my case to an attorney," she said. "Especially when I'm just going on a gut feeling, but here's why I'm not ready to let this go just yet. Tad Brewster willingly turned over his phone at the interview. And since we already have the transcripts from Kerimides's phone, the forensics team that first went over the embalming area must have located it without much trouble."

Guy set his pile of documents aside and rose to pick up a cookie. "Would that not be all the more reason why neither had anything to cover up?"

"I don't disagree," Syd replied. "But you scrutinized the phone calls as well as the texts and emails around those dates Dan Sheridan thought he'd overheard Brewster's mysterious phone call, and you found nothing of a personal nature. Right?"

"Right."

"Nor did you, Kat? Right?"

"Correct," Kat replied. "What are you getting at?"

"You two didn't interview Sheridan. He was so sure Brewster was talking to someone about something very private, even if it wasn't Kerimides. One of us should have found that call or calls on the transcripts."

"Then Sheridan remembered wrong," Kat said. "Or maybe it was a different date."

"Or was lying," Guy said.

"But why? Why would Sheridan lie or be confused about what he heard and when?"

Guy returned to his former seat across from her. "Does he

have something against Brewster and wants to throw suspicion on him?"

"It didn't seem like he did when we talked to him. He only brought up overhearing the call when we pushed," Syd said.

"Maybe that was for effect," Guy said. "It happened to me more than once with witnesses who acted like they had to be encouraged to say something against a peer."

"I would like to think I'm a better judge of character than that."

"Syd is pretty good at lie detecting," Kat said.

Guy leaned his jaw into his templed hands. "I'm sure you are. I was just suggesting an alternative version of his story."

Kat went on. "I believe you, Syd. At least, I believe how strongly you believe what Dan Sheridan told you. I'd say we need to interview him again and confront him with our findings."

"Or lack thereof," Guy added.

As they packed up their documents, Kat offered to send some of the goodies home with Guy. "If I know Micki, she'd appreciate your bringing home a late-night snack, even though you'll be eating here later this afternoon."

"Don't mind me," Syd said. "I cook and bake almost as little as Micki."

Kat had to laugh. "Of course, Syd. Please, help yourself. I'm sure Trip will be starved when he and Beau get back from Shasta."

"THANKS FOR MEETING WITH US," Beau told John Seymour, the

substitute mortician from Shasta, as soon as he and Trip were settled in the mortician's office.

Seymour wore his hair shoulder-length, silver having taken over three-fourths of his head, dark brown still fighting for life around the back edges. Of moderate height, brown eyes set wide apart with shaggy white brows, he appeared to be in his mid-fifties. He was dressed in a black T-shirt sporting a logo that said "Shasta Forever" over a pair of well-worn blue jeans. "I need to get back to one of my clients once we're done talking. Business has tripled since Kerimides's death."

"We'll keep that in mind," Beau said. He did a quick overview of their part in the investigation and then began his questions. "How would you describe the victim, Gordon Kerimides?"

"Hardly knew him. My only contact was through emails notifying me when he needed my services. He didn't attend meetings of other area morticians. His sister-in-law attends those."

"How often did you sub for him?"

"Not enough that I could live on that income," Seymour replied. "Maybe once every six months? He seems to have been pretty healthy, or he worked through whatever ailments besieged him."

"How would you describe your relationship with him?" Trip asked.

"Cordial? He never complained about my work."

"How did you find the work area?"

Seymour screwed up his face. "Not sure what you mean. Was it up-to-date? Yes, Kerimides made sure he had the best equipment and embalming supplies. Did it have an efficient layout? Yes, I wouldn't expect less from the guy. That the kind of thing you want to know about?"

"Among other things," Trip replied. "You didn't notice anything unusual?"

"I wasn't ever there long enough to study my surroundings. Even when Kerimides was gone for one reason or another, I didn't go over unless there was a client needing attention. I prepared the body and left. If anything, I noticed an abundance of some supplies as I was working."

"What kind of supplies?" Trip continued.

Seymour closed his eyes briefly, trying to recall. "Distilled water, for one. I don't even use the stuff in my process. And sodium hydroxide, I think. I barely glanced at it, just filed away the question, 'What does he use that for?' But you have to keep in mind, each of us tends to develop our own methods. As long as they're within the bounds of professional standards and the law, deviations are okay."

"Anything else you remember that might have been unusual?"

Seymour actually scratched his head. "I take it you know about his office? When I first starting filling in for him, he warned me in an email that his office was off-limits. If I needed a bathroom, there was one down the hall. Of course I couldn't resist taking a peek. Mainly curious. Not all of us have our own offices away from the main office. Turns out, this was more than an office. There was also a day bed, refrigerator, hot plate and microwave in there. He also kept some clothes there.

"I'd heard about his need for privacy, so this home-away-from-home suggested he stayed there for more than cases that took him into the early morning hours. I left the computer alone. I recorded all the necessary data on my phone and sent it to him from that. But that didn't stop me from snooping through the personal items I found. Long story short, I found a black silk thong amongst several other pairs of boxers."

He eyed Trip and Beau like he was expecting them to pick up on whatever he was inferring.

"Okay?" Beau replied, taking the bait. "Are you suggesting he occasionally varied his underwear?"

"I forgot to mention the thong was a smaller size than the other items," Seymour told them, one eyebrow raised.

"Spit it out, man," Trip said. If Seymour had suspicions about Kerimides's private life, he needed to go on record rather than leaving it to them to speculate.

"I don't like to speak ill of the dead. But in this case, since you're attempting to learn more about the man, that thong suggests someone else had spent time in that room."

"A woman?"

Seymour shook his head. "Too large, although too small for Kerimides, judging by the other clothes in that room, since I'd never met the guy."

"You're telling us another man spent time in that room?" Beau said. "And what? Left them behind as a souvenir?"

The mortician straightened his shoulders. "I'm not telling you anything. You asked me if I'd noticed anything unusual, and I answered your question." He came to his feet. "Now I really must get back to my client."

Their signal to leave.

"That comment about the sodium hydroxide and distilled water confirmed what Marianne and Micki found in Kerimides's embalming area," Beau told Trip on their way back to town. "She couldn't wait until our group get-together later today to let me know."

"Too bad Seymour either didn't know or didn't want to say what that meant," Trip replied.

"Strange arrangement, wouldn't you say, working for someone you've never met and only getting your instructions by email?"

"Maybe at one time," Beau said, "but not unusual in this day and age. Especially since his services weren't needed very often."

"What about the elephant in the room? The black silk thong?" Trip asked.

"What do you think?" Beau asked rather than replying.

"Coward."

"No, I don't want to leap too fast to what could easily be a wrong conclusion."

"But it's okay for me to take that leap?" Trip replied jokingly. "Okay, I'll give it a shot. Actually three shots. First, what Seymour wanted us to get, Kerimides had entertained a man in his private quarters at one time. But those skivvies could mean a lot of things. For another, they could've belonged to Kerimides. Too small when compared to his other sizes? Maybe, but he could've gotten some kind of thrill from wearing something so tight. Or finally, he could've taken them from a body for any number of reasons."

"Good assessment, though somewhat grisly. Let's not make too much of this. Not right now, anyhow. But sometimes one detail like that can turn a case on its heels."

"Let's see what the others think of it, especially the women," Trip said.

Chapter Twenty

Since they all finished their follow-up interviews by mid-afternoon, the group met early at Kat's house. Greta had returned home an hour before, still buzzed from her lunch with friends and carrying several shopping bags. Guy, Syd and Kat had barely touched the goodies she'd left for them. Nonetheless, she augmented what remained with a light supper for the full team to consume while they consumed each other's findings.

"We learned the name of the substitute mortician, John Seymour over in Shasta," Micki said. "I already texted his name to Trip."

"And Beau and I just got back from seeing him," Trip told the group. "We'll report on that visit once the rest of you have your say."

"We also got the name of the company that picks up the waste from the embalming area," Marianne said. "It's Torrance Waste Management. Stacia Kerimides didn't know who the pickup person was. Her brother-in-law took care of all their dealings with the company."

"We called the company as soon as we concluded our

meeting with Stacia," Micki continued. "Apparently only one of their people had been picking up the funeral home's waste for the last year or so. A guy by the name of Bob Terry."

Rick made a notation on the whiteboard. "Check out Bob Terry."

Micki described the general layout of the funeral home's basement. "We only toured the embalming area. If necessary, someone can return to tour the custodial and storage parts of the business."

"Was there anything strange or unusual in the embalming area?" Rick asked.

"That's why we asked Stacia to accompany us," Marianne said. "Neither of us had ever seen an embalming room. The very thought of what went on there, though absolutely necessary, wasn't part of our mindset. Anything we witnessed on our own could've struck us as strange but simply been part of the process. That's why it was critical we have Stacia with us. She would be able to identify whatever was out of place or missing."

"And?" Syd said, her impatience showing.

"Keep in mind, Stacia hadn't been in that room in years," Marianne said. "It was almost like she was experiencing it for the first time, just like us. She spotted two items among the embalming supplies that surprised her, sodium hydroxide and distilled water."

Trip broke into her story. "That's what John Seymour, the substitute mortician from Shasta, told us! Did she say what she thought they were doing there?"

"No. I got the impression she was truly thrown to see them. The room wasn't that large. Space was at a premium.

So why would he take up valuable space with items that weren't needed?"

Rick noted sodium hydroxide and distilled water on the whiteboard.

"Afterwards, I did a little more research about sodium hydroxide," Marianne added. "It's been a while since I dealt with chemicals on a daily basis. In liquid form, it's used throughout industry to tone down the pH in various products. As a solid, it's highly toxic. I'm not a chemist, so I didn't understand all I read. Suffice it to say, it's a commonly used additive."

"Any other surprises?" Rick asked.

"Not so much a surprise as a comment when she noted the number of waste containers he'd been stocking. Double from what there should be, according to Stacia. It wasn't just the number. It was also that the labeling on some was a different color, black rather than red. Red apparently means dangerous in that world. So why the different labeling? Again, she couldn't offer an explanation."

"Those two observations could be critical," Trip said, "since they were confirmed by Seymour. Which pretty much sums up what we learned from our visit."

"Other than the fact he'd never met Kerimides in person. Kerimides sent him an email whenever his services were needed," Beau added. "Not totally unheard of in this technical age, but it's one more sign of his need for privacy."

Micki was seated on the room's long sofa next to Guy with Kat on her other side. "I checked out Kerimides's office while Marianne and Stacia finished up their review of the embalming room," Micki said. "There wasn't much to see, although *office* is a misnomer. His computer was there along with some office supplies and a filing cabinet, but the rest was a like a studio apartment," she said, going into a brief rundown of the contents.

"That's all?" Rick asked when she finished.

Micki and Marianne exchanged looks.

"Okay, true confession time," Micki said with resignation. "I was somewhat, uh, overwhelmed by what I saw in the embalming room. I had to leave before I either puked or fainted. Deputy Martinez took me to Kerimides's office, which was just down the hall, and stayed with me while I recovered. Over half my time in that room was spent spread out on the day bed, eyes closed."

Although he'd been sitting next to her, Guy put a protective arm around her shoulders. "Are you okay now?"

"My ego is still recovering, but yes, physically I'm fine. I owe Marianne an apology. Before we got there, I was afraid the experience would be too much for her. Then I …"

"It happened, Mick. It's over," Marianne said, patting her hand.

"You said you found some of Kerimides's clothes in that room," Trip said to Micki. "Did you discover anything unusual about them?"

Micki cocked her head. "Sorry. I guess I should have done more peeking while I was in there, but I didn't feel up to it. Why do you ask?"

Beau glanced at Trip. "Guess this is as good a time as any to share one more tidbit we learned from the substitute mortician. You tell them."

Trip mouthed something that looked like "coward" to Marianne.

"In his snooping Seymour found a black silk thong. In a

smaller size than Kerimides's other underthings. We were hoping you could confirm its existence," Trip said.

"Could Seymour tell if it was a woman's or man's thong?" Micki asked.

"How could one tell?" Beau said.

The rest of them gasped, even Marianne, who knew better. Who knew her husband knew better, too, if he'd think about it a minute.

"Even I can answer that one," Guy replied. "And I'm no detective like you folks." He paused to let that claim sink in. "But then, I've never owned a thong, black silk or otherwise."

A Mona Lisa-esque smile came over Micki's face.

"Oh," Beau returned as Marianne rolled her eyes.

"How about the phone transcripts for Brewster and Kerimides?" Rick asked. "What did you guys find?"

"In a word, nothing," Guy answered.

"Oh," Rick replied.

"Guy's a little disappointed," Kat tried to explain. "Our task was mainly to check out the dates when Sheridan thought he'd overheard Tad Brewster on private calls and also identify anything else of interest in their phone calls, emails and texts. And like he said, we didn't find anything."

"Too bad. I really thought there might be something there," Rick said. "Oh well, moving on."

"Wait!" Syd cried. "Before we dismiss that idea of private phone calls altogether, let's talk about why we came up with zero."

"Okay?" Rick replied. "Did you not get the full group?"

"Yes, at least I think so. It's just that I really believed Dan Sheridan when he claimed to have overheard Brewster talking to someone privately."

"I agree with Syd," Trip said. "The guy really sounded genuine."

"If he was, why didn't you guys find any evidence of them?" Rick asked.

An idea played through Marianne's brain as the others discussed the transcripts. She'd learned not to discount Syd. Syd knew her stuff. "Could the calls have been deleted?" she asked.

"Is that even possible? I always heard you couldn't delete call data completely," Guy said.

"I'm no expert, but my understanding is that you have to drill deep to find it, but it can be done," Rick said.

"Does the sheriff have the ability to do that?" Marianne asked.

"Why are you so interested?" Guy asked.

"Because when Beau and I interviewed him, he willingly handed his phone to Deputy Hastings. Only someone would do that who hadn't made such calls or had deleted and buried them so deep no one except experts could find them."

She paused before going on. "Or here's another possibility, a hypothesis if you will. They made their calls on disposable phones. Burners, if you will."

"Burner phones? That's brilliant," Syd said.

"Not so fast," Guy said. "Have you been watching too many police dramas?"

"Bear with me as I walk you through this," Marianne said, playing around with the idea. "Let's say Kerimides did have a burner phone. We've heard repeatedly that he was a private person, so having one of those phones would fit the mold."

"Why would he need one when he handled his everyday business either by text or email? Less so by phone, as you guys found in his transcripts," Rick asked.

Challenged, Marianne reached for an explanation. "For highly personal calls like Dan Sheridan might have over-heard, or to cover up unlawful activities." As if those ideas weren't solid enough, she took one more stab at her emerging theory. "That black thong the sub mortician found? What if it belonged to someone else? A man."

"Let me see if I'm following you," Micki said. "The very private Kerimides could have been covering up an affair with a man? You got all that from the fact there was nothing on those transcripts and a thong?" Micki, usually the first to leap to crazy ideas, was clearly skeptical.

"I told you it was just a hypothesis. But it fits with Syd and Trip's strong belief that Sheridan was sincere."

"What are you proposing, Marianne?" Rick asked. "That we search Kerimides's and Brewster's living quarters again?"

"Would Sheriff Quinn go along with it?" she asked.

"If I sell it well enough," he replied. "But I need to be convinced first."

"What more do you need to know?" she asked.

"Other than Kerimides being involved with a man, you also suggested that Kerimides might have been involved with something shady. This is me taking as big a leap as you have. What if there really was something odd about the sodium hydroxide, distilled water and extra waste containers? We need to brainstorm what that could've been."

"I'm the scientist of the group. Let me call some people,"

Marianne said, keeping her earlier thought to herself until she'd had a chance to look into it further.

"We need to track down that guy from the waste management company, Bob Terry," Syd said. "Besides possibly having some connections to those chemicals and waste containers, he's the last interview to check off our list."

"I'll get the ball rolling with Quinn for a warrant to search Brewster's house for a burner phone. But just in case there's anything to this thong thing, we'll work it in to allow us to go through his wardrobe."

"Thanks, Rick," Marianne said, pleased he hadn't totally dismissed her hypothesis.

"We'll see if the sister-in-law will give us access again to the embalming area, especially the office and also his condo, or if we'll need a warrant. Micki, it's up to you if you want to skip a return."

She shook her head ferociously. "No, now that I know what to expect, I want to redeem my earlier meltdown."

Finally, Rick turned to Syd, Trip and Beau. "We need to talk to the guy from Torrance Waste Management, Bob Terry. But don't call him in advance. We may have already tipped our hand by calling to get his name. If as Marianne has suggested, Kerimides was involved in something illegal, we don't want Terry skipping town if he was somehow tied up in it.

"Where does that leave us?" he continued. "Marianne and Micki will check out Kerimides's quarters at the funeral home. Syd, Trip and Beau will track down Bob Terry. Make sure one of the deputies is with you, since you have no idea who this guy is. Marianne will talk to her contacts in the world of chemistry. Trip, Guy and I will check out Kerimides's condo."

"Does the fact we're not talking to the others again mean we've eliminated them and now we're just considering Brewster and Bob Terry?" Marianne asked.

Rick surveyed the group. "What do the rest of you think?"

"We've been at this all of two days," Syd replied. "I'm not ready to check anyone off the list just yet. Not until we've completed the assignments you just gave us."

"Agreed. Anything else we need to cover now?" Rick asked.

"Weren't Quinn's people working on the financial data of those we've interviewed?" Trip, the former banker, asked.

"I'll check on that, too," Rick replied. "Thanks, everyone, for your efforts today. We've made a lot of headway with this case. Tomorrow we'll make more."

Chapter Twenty-One

"You're sure you're up to doing this again?" Marianne asked Micki as they joined Stacia Kerimides and Deputy Martinez in the funeral home's lobby the following morning.

"Yes. I shouldn't have eaten pancakes for breakfast yesterday, but Guy surprised me by making breakfast before he joined Marianne to go through those transcripts," Micki replied. "I limited myself to a piece of toast and half a cup of coffee today." Her swagger was back today, so hopefully it remained as they resumed their tour.

Stacia Kerimides gave them permission to search the embalming suite even though Deputy Martinez handed her a search warrant. "As much as I want to learn who killed my brother-in-law," she said, "I hope these tours of the facility are coming to an end. Not just because I want to reopen, but they are taking up a considerable amount of my time."

"Understood," Marianne told her, assuming her most diplomatic persona.

"As you saw yesterday, the embalming area is quite organized despite the hostility that apparently went on down there before Gordon was killed. I don't want to see it messed up any further."

"That's why your presence is required," Micki said.

"But it's dangerous! You could be exposing yourselves to hazardous chemicals."

"We brought protective gloves and masks for all of us," Marianne said.

"Are you supporting this, Deputy?" Stacia asked Martinez.

"In particular, we're looking for a second phone. Unless you already know where it is?" Martinez said.

Stacia stared at them like they'd just turned into alien beings. "Another phone? I never saw one or knew about one. Why do think he had one?"

"The warrant details the reasons behind this search, if you want to read it now," Martinez replied. "We'll hold up to allow you time to review it," Martinez said.

Scowling, Stacia took a minute to review the document. "This says you're looking for a conversation Gordon supposedly had with someone that wasn't found in the transcripts of his phone calls, so you've decided there must be another phone. And you convinced a judge to sign this based on this flimsy rationale?"

"I can't comment on the warrant, Mrs. Kerimides," Martinez said evenly. "My job is to see that it is served and followed."

Although she let them proceed toward the embalming area, Stacia wasn't done commenting. "Gordon was a very private person. I can see why a private phone might appeal to him, but for what reason?"

No one answered her question. Instead, the other three women put on their protective gloves and masks and began examining the various contents of the room. Stacia hung in the background eyeing their every move.

They'd been at it fifteen minutes when Micki stopped and turned to Stacia. "If he had a second phone, where do you think he'd put it? Would he hide it or leave it in plain sight, at least for his eyes?"

Stacia shrugged. "I don't know why you ask me. I didn't know he had one, if he even did." But that didn't prevent her from searching the room with her eyes. The idea of her brother-in-law keeping a burner phone apparently intrigued her.

At the forty-minute mark, Marianne and Micki agreed the embalming room had not yielded a second phone. And the smell was getting to them.

The staging room went quicker, although once again Micki had to take a deep breath when Stacia opened the cooler for them. "I'm showing you this just so you can check it off your list, but I don't know how a phone would survive the cold," she told them.

In the office, they paid particular attention to the clothing items they found in a bureau—including the black silk thong—the closet, the filing cabinet and the drawers in his desk. Eleven minutes into the search of the office, they found the second phone, tucked between two cereal boxes.

Martinez quickly whipped out an evidence bag. "I'll take that, ladies."

"Should we keep looking, in case he had a backup?" Marianne asked.

"A backup? Really?" Stacia said. "Do you think he was a spy or something?"

The other three didn't reply. As little as they knew about

the dead man even after spending the last few days digging into his life, his being a spy wasn't beyond the impossible.

"Let's see what we find on this phone first," Martinez said. "You have every right to continue looking on your own," she told Stacia, "but anything you find, you have to report to me. The warrant spells that out."

Stacia led them back upstairs and then went back to her office as they made their way to the front entrance.

"How soon do you think she'll go back down there?" Micki asked the other two.

"You really think she'd go?" Marianne asked.

"I'm not supposed to speculate, but off the record, I'd give her five minutes. Long enough to make sure we've left."

"Deputy Martinez—Pilar—even though this investigation may not be over, we want you to know how much we appreciate all you've done to help us thus far," Marianne said as they were about to part.

"The same goes for me," Micki added. "Especially yesterday, when I let the environment get to me. You've been such a professional, and you are a great example of women in law enforcement."

Martinez briefly bowed her head. "Thank you both." With that, she pivoted and quickly jumped into her vehicle and took off.

"Your hunch paid off," Micki said once she pulled her car away from the funeral home. "I don't know if I would have put two and two together like that. Guy will be gobsmacked. After our group meeting yesterday, he confided that he'd gone along with you because you'd seemed so sure of your theory, he didn't want to completely write it off, even though he did try to discourage you."

"I'm so pumped. Should we take another walk?"

"You're kidding, I hope?" Micki shot back.

Marianne laughed. "Of course. Let's go have the rest of that breakfast you skipped to celebrate. Then I've got some calls to make to some chemists I know."

"WAS THIS GUY A MONK?" Trip asked as he, Rick and Guy searched Kerimides's condo. "There's hardly any furniture and absolutely no decorations."

"That's right, you weren't with us the first time we checked this place out," Guy said. "From what we heard from Micki and Marianne, he seemed to spend more time in his office at the funeral home than here."

"Wait till you see the kitchen. Hardly kept any food items around. We surmised that he ordered in whatever meals he took here," Rick said.

"That should make searching for a burner phone easy," Trip replied.

"From the standpoint of there being very little to see, yes," Rick said. "But that doesn't dismiss secret compartments. And they're much harder to find."

"Do we have to tap walls?" Trip asked.

"Something like that," Rick responded.

"Too bad none of us are carpenters," Guy said. "Then we'd at least have some idea what we're doing."

Nonetheless, the three of them each chose a wall to examine and set off to look for buried treasure. During the next fifteen minutes soft tapping sounds could be heard throughout the place.

"Find anything?" Rick asked from the door of the bedroom as Trip was making his way over the floor.

Trip swiveled around to face him. "No dust bunnies, candy wrappers, nothing. Makes me wonder if Kerimides wore a paper gown while here. You know, like the kind the nurse in the doctor's office makes you wear for your annual examination."

"Guy and I came up with the same negative results. But not to worry. He and I both received calls just now from Micki and Marianne. They had more luck. The deputy took the burner phone into her custody to see what their forensics people can find."

Trip came to his feet, rubbing his knees once aright. "Glad someone's search wasn't in vain."

"We might still be successful ourselves. I just received a text from Quinn. The warrant to search Brewster's place has been approved. Deputy Martinez will meet us there."

Chapter Twenty-Two

"I don't understand," Tad Brewster said to Deputy Martinez after she'd handed him the warrant. "This says you're looking for a phone. I already gave my phone to the other deputy. And I understand you've already gone through a transcript of my calls for the last year or so."

"Feel free to call your attorney if you don't understand it, sir," Martinez said. "Or just settle back and let us search."

"All of you?"

"I can assure you all three of these gentlemen know what they are doing. Mr. Formero is the former sheriff who has recently opened his own private investigation agency. Mr. Bonner is being trained as an investigative intern, and Mr. Whitney is an attorney."

"That's right. My earlier pair of visitors were from your agency, Formero. And now the big cheese is here for another go-round. I'd feel flattered if this wasn't such a huge waste of your time and mine."

"Perhaps you'd like to follow through on my suggestion?" Martinez said, politely stern. "Be seated somewhere out of the way while we complete our task."

Brewster shrugged. "Fine. Excuse the dishes in the sink. I didn't clean up after dinner last night."

With that, they left him seated in his living room on the first floor while they separated to search in pairs after putting on the disposable gloves Martinez had brought along. Guy and Martinez took the first floor, three bedrooms, the kitchen and dining area, two bathrooms, and the living room, where Brewster stared daggers at them.

Rick and Trip drew the basement, which included Brewster's studio and office, a small kitchenette, another bedroom and bath.

"Those are my personal papers you're rifling through," Brewster said to Trip from the doorway of his office, having left his observation post upstairs.

"I'm not the IRS," Trip replied. "I'm just moving things around enough to see if a phone might be buried under these stacks of documents. Thought you were content to stay upstairs. Something down here you don't want us to see?"

"There's a lot I don't want you to see because it's technically property of my clients and thus confidential."

"If you're going to watch my every move, maybe you should pull up a chair," Trip said. "Make yourself more comfortable."

"I'm okay here where I can see what both of you are doing."

"Suit yourself."

If there was a second phone to be found, it must be downstairs. Brewster would've stayed upstairs, which he tried to do at first, but that must've been a ruse to throw them off. Trip slowed down his search. Didn't want to miss something.

He scanned the desktop carefully. Nothing. The same

for the drawers, which included mainly office supplies. Next, he went over and through the credenza behind the desk. Stacks of books and more documents but still nothing. The same for the filing cabinets full of proposal folders.

As much as he attempted to appear disinterested, Brewster was giving off vibes that suggested exactly the opposite. He made a show of attempting to read an architectural magazine but hardly turned any pages because he kept looking over at Trip.

Trip was just about finished with this office, but something told him he was getting hot. Perhaps the fact that Brewster had ended the pretense of studying the magazine and had set it aside to simply stare at Trip.

Trip got down on his knees and looked under the knee-hole. Still nothing. Then he looked under the main office chair and the two visitor chairs.

Brewster's breathing increased. Another sign Trip was getting closer.

Finally, Trip sat in Brewster's chair. Elbows on desktop, he leaned forward and clasped his hands.

"What are you doing?" Brewster's volume increased.

"At the moment, trying to think like you. Not easy."

"Hey! You're not supposed to insult me while you search."

"My apologies. No offense intended. I've never used a second phone. I'm trying to figure out where I'd put one if I needed to keep it nearby but out of the way. I'd ask you, but I don't want to put you in a more awkward position than you already are." He paused, considered his last words. "On second thought, I will. Where is your burner phone, Mr. Brewster?"

Brewster didn't reply, although he did offer a disgusted look.

"That's okay. I get it. For some reason, you don't want anyone else to know about your private life."

"No, I just don't appreciate a sheriff's deputy and amateurs going through my personal things."

"You could end your discomfort right now and tell me where I can find it," Trip said.

Brewster simply continued to stare at him.

Okay, the guy planned to gut this out, gambling that their search would turn up nothing. Too bad. They were too close to give up now.

Back to pretending to be Brewster. Where would he put a burner phone? His gut was telling him this was the place, even though he'd been through everything in sight. And out of sight, or had he checked everywhere? He opened all the side drawers again, feeling around for secret compartments. Still no luck.

That left only the main drawer above the kneehole. Brewster was an architect. They knew how to utilize space to their advantage. Had he worked some kind of magic here?

Trip carefully moved around the few items in the drawer: ballpoint pens, a stack of sticky note pads, paper clips, batteries and a pair of scissors. Nothing.

A secret compartment on one of the sides? No.

In the space above the drawer and under the desktop? Once again, zero. Wait! He felt it way at the back, lodged between two prongs coming down from below the desktop.

"Rick!"

In his excitement at finding the phone, he shifted his attention from Brewster to removing the phone. In that instant, Brewster shot from where he'd been leaning against the door, jumped on top of Trip and grabbed his hand away from the drawer.

"Martinez!" Rick yelled from the other room but within a second was on top of Brewster, peeling him away from Trip.

In the melee, the drawer slammed against Trip's right forearm. He didn't feel the pain until Martinez was slipping her handcuffs on Brewster and leading him out of the room. She stayed in the studio with him while Rick helped Trip remove his arm from the drawer.

"You okay?" Rick asked.

Trip grasped his right forearm with his left hand as he sucked in a breath. "I've been better. But we found it, man! You'll have to do the honors, though. I'm sorta out of commission at the moment."

"Why's Brewster in handcuffs?" Guy asked, rushing into the office.

"Trip apparently struck gold, and Brewster tried to stop him," Rick said.

"Looks like you got injured in the offing," Guy said, noting Trip still grasping his arm. "Should I call an ambulance?"

"Don't you dare!" Trip cried. "At least not until we're sure I found the real thing."

"Then sit down over there while I try to remove this thing. It's in here pretty tight. Brewster must have used it mainly to make calls. There's no telling how long it would take to get to it if it rang." Two seconds later, Rick held the phone in his hand. "Locked."

"We need Brewster to open it," Trip said.

"Are you in good enough shape for us to approach him now?" Rick asked him.

Trip bit a lip but nodded. "This is too important for me to give in to a little pain."

"Martinez should be party to this, too," Rick said. "Let's move out to the studio, where there's more room."

"Anything you want to tell us before we check out this phone?" Rick asked Brewster once they were all assembled in the studio.

"You had no right to handcuff me," Brewster replied.

"You struck an officially sanctioned member of this search party," Rick returned.

"And maybe broke my arm," Trip threw in.

Brewster snorted.

"Deputy Martinez?" Rick asked. "What's your assessment? Can the cuffs be removed while we quiz him about this phone?"

Martinez turned to Brewster. "It's up to you, Mr. Brewster. I'll consider not arresting you for assaulting Mr. Bonner if you help us find what we're seeking."

Brewster, apparently realizing his best option was to cooperate, nodded.

"Please say you will cooperate out loud," Martinez said, more firmly than before.

Brewster heaved a sigh. "Fine. Yes. I will cooperate." Rick handed him his phone long enough for Brewster to enter the code to unlock the phone then give it back to Rick.

"We'll start with the most recent text entry and go back," Rick said, proceeding. "Well, look here. It's from someone called Gordo to you. *Sorry about tonight.*

"You to Gordo: *Second time this week. Business that heavy?*

"Gordo: *Business, yeah. A meeting came up I can't avoid.*

"You: *All night? I can come late.*

"Gordo: *That won't work.*

"You: *Are you breaking up with me?*

"Gordo: *No, babe. Not at all. I've just got to do this.*

"Let's stop there for now," Rick said. "Care to comment, Brewster? Because unless you claim this exchange was with someone other than Gordon Kerimides, this suggests you and he were lovers."

The three non-law-enforcement searchers waited for Brewster to say something while Martinez admired her set of handcuffs.

"I guess there's no point hiding it any longer. He's the one who insisted we keep our relationship quiet. Said no one would trust a gay mortician with their loved ones. Stupid, I know, but he convinced me it wouldn't be good for me on the council either."

"Which is why the burner phones?" Guy asked.

"Yeah. Gordon thrived on the secrecy. Sometimes I suspected he was more into that than our relationship. It's only been since his death that I've begun to wonder if he wasn't using his phone for other reasons as well."

"Other reasons?" Trip asked.

"You read it yourself. He kept calling off our times together, even though I was willing to come late and stay until morning."

"You wouldn't happen to own a ..." Trip was about to ask until Guy shook his head.

"We were just about to call you upstairs when we were summoned downstairs," Guy said. He reached in his pants pocket and pulled out a scrap of black silk.

"You went through my underwear drawer?" Brewster asked, his face turning red.

"Where better to hide a burner phone?" Guy returned.

"Getting back to you and Kerimides," Rick said, "did you suspect he was seeing someone else?"

"I did at first until I did my own stakeout. Check the date on that exchange of texts. It's the same date as the night he was murdered."

"You saw his murderer?" Trip asked.

"Not exactly. It was a dark night. I had to watch from that field where they want the dog park, far enough away so I wouldn't be seen. He or she parked a van at the back entrance, the same one I used when I stayed over."

"What time was it?" Rick asked.

"After midnight. When he opened the door, he didn't seem like he was greeting my rival. I thought I heard him say, 'This is the last time, Barry.' Whoever this Barry was pushed him inside. It didn't look like they were cheating on me, but I wasn't sure what was going on. I waited there another half hour or more hoping I could figure it out or gather up the courage to confront them. I was about to give up when the door opened again and whoever it was emerged. No Gordon. But the stranger was carrying what seemed like gallon containers of something, which they quickly loaded in the back of the vehicle. Whoever it was went back two more times for more of the same."

"What time did he leave?" Trip asked.

"By then it was around two."

"Why didn't you tell Mr. and Mrs. Putnam about what you'd seen when they interviewed you the other day?" Rick asked.

"And admit to spying on my lover at midnight from the empty field I'd been trying to keep from becoming a dog park simply to please my lover? With Gordo gone, my seat on the council has become more important to me than ever."

"Let's go back to what you overheard. 'This is the last time, Barry.' Are you sure that's what you heard?" Rick asked.

Brewster's brow furrowed up. "Pretty sure, although I was far enough away I couldn't hear clearly. That's part of why I hung around. If he did have something going with that person and this was the last time, maybe we could salvage things between us."

"Could it have been Jerry? Or Gary? Or Larry, Cary or Terry?"

Brewster rubbed his jaw. "I thought I heard Barry, but I suppose it could have been one of those others you listed."

Rick and the others exchanged glances. They had to inform the rest of the team. Time was of the essence.

"Deputy Martinez will keep your phone for now," Rick told Brewster. "If she agrees, that's all we need from you right now. But don't go anywhere." For all they knew, given this latest evidence, Brewster still could have gone back and killed his lover after the mysterious Barry left.

"Yeah, sure."

They were upstairs and almost at the front door when Brewster called out to them. "Wait! I believe you have something else of mine. Surely you don't need it?"

Guy reluctantly reached in his pocket and handed the scrap of black silk to Brewster.

Chapter Twenty-Three

"How much longer do we give this guy to return from his job?" Beau asked Syd and Deputy Hastings as they sat parked in front of Torrance Waste Management.

Even though they'd arrived early, at eight that morning, Bob Terry had already left to pick up three loads, or so the dispatcher they talked with first had told them. The manager echoed the same story. "Why do you want to speak with him?" he'd asked.

"Police business, sir," Hastings had told him. "And it would be in the best interest of you and the rest of your people," he said, glancing at the dispatcher, "not to let him know we're here." He paused for effect. "Is that clear?"

This was the first time Syd had worked with Hastings. For once, she was glad to have a deputy with them. Hastings could flex his official muscles when the rest of the team couldn't.

The manager told the dispatcher to estimate what time Terry would show up. "He's on three regular pickups," the dispatcher said. "He's usually back around now."

"Thanks," Beau said. "We'll wait in the car."

But after an hour, when Terry still hadn't shown up, they went back in and straight to the manager this time. Hastings took the lead, first introducing himself and then Syd and Beau. "Mr. Terry is a person of interest in a homicide case we're investigating. It's imperative we speak with him as soon as possible."

"Is he in trouble?"

"Sorry, I can't answer that," Hastings replied.

"Let's talk in my office," the manager said. "I'm George Parker, by the way."

Hastings and company followed Parker down a hallway and into a small office.

"Look, I'm not just curious," Parker said. "I need to know if any of my people are in trouble with the law because of the nature of my business."

The three took chairs in the office, but no one responded.

"I might know something about this guy that could help your investigation."

Hastings again took the lead. "Okay? What do you know about Bob Terry?"

"For starters, the guy's a closed book. I don't trust him. He's hiding something."

"Why do you say that?" Hastings asked.

"Vehicles like ours can be tempting to guys looking to make extra money. So we track weight load and travel miles among other things to ensure our drivers aren't involved in extracurricular activities. Terry's numbers haven't been adding up for several months, but every time I've confronted him, he's had some excuse or another. Not very good reasons but just sound enough I didn't force the issue or fire him. But if he's got himself involved in something illegal, I need to know. I gotta protect my business and my clients."

Deputy Hastings turned to Beau and Syd. "Go ahead. You tell him."

Beau gave Parker an overview of Kerimides's death and their investigation. "Because the victim led such a private life with so few contacts with others, we're looking closely at anyone who might be part of that limited group. It appears Terry was one of them."

"The waste pickup occurred at the back entrance, which is located in the most private part of the building," Syd added.

Parker cocked his head. "You think Terry was involved in something illegal that involved Kerimides?"

"It's only a possibility," Beau replied. "That's why we want to talk to him."

He exchanged a look with Syd as if to ask how much of their theory they should share.

"You mentioned some discrepancies in weight loads Terry carried. Is it possible those were the result of hauling more than just one or two waste containers?" she asked.

The manager considered. "I suppose that could account for it. A typical waste container from the funeral home runs between seven and fifteen pounds. An additional container might add maybe fifteen to twenty pounds more. That might account for the weight difference. But surely that additional weight hasn't been waste?"

"We don't know," Beau answered. "We thought you might have an idea."

Parker shook his head. "Surely you don't think I've been involved?"

"We have to ask," Beau said.

"I have no idea what Terry has been up to, if he has even been doing something illegal. If he has been involved in something other than his assigned job duties, he may have been removing something from the building, which would account for the extra weight."

"What about the additional miles he clocked?" Syd asked. "How much farther did he travel on his trips?"

"Between ten and twenty miles each trip."

"Those extra miles could have taken him anywhere within town or the outskirts," Beau said. "Maybe that's why he isn't back yet today, although there's been no business from the funeral home since Kerimides died."

The manager made a face. "If you think he's dirty, maybe that goes beyond just the funeral home."

"Is he frequently late finishing his runs?" Syd asked.

"Occasionally, but not this late." He closed his eyes briefly, running something through his head. "After a couple times of those extra miles, I put a tracker on his vehicle."

That got Hastings's attention. "A tracker?" he said a little too loudly.

"That's not against the law," Parker quickly said. "The vehicle belongs to the business, and I'm in charge of the business."

Hastings leaned forward. "How often do you check it?"

"I did every day for a while, but nothing out of the ordinary showed up, so I stopped checking so often. I even thought maybe he'd found it and was deliberately staying clean."

"Could you check it now?" Syd asked. Why hadn't he mentioned the tracker in the first place?

"You sure have reason," Beau added. "As late as he is."

Parker moved over to his laptop and keyed in instructions. "This gizmo lets me pinpoint his exact location or download a map tracing his moves for any given period of time." He waited, and they all held their collective breath. Parker sat back and pointed to the screen. "And there he is. Or at least the vehicle."

Three heads popped over his shoulder.

"What are we looking at?" Syd asked.

"That blue dot is his vehicle. It's parked just inside the hazardous waste landfill on the outskirts of town."

"Any way of knowing if he's there too?" Beau asked.

"Nah. All I've cared about has been the vehicle, making sure I knew where it was at all times."

Syd straightened up and pulled Hastings aside. "Should we go there and confront him?" she asked in a lowered voice.

"Have you ever seen one of those places?" Hastings asked her.

"Well, no."

"They go on forever, full of barrels and barrels of discarded waste or worse, garbage bags or sometimes just open discard. They're not called *hazardous* for nothing."

"He's right, ma'am," Parker said, apparently having overheard. "For all we know, he learned you're on to him and is on his way out of town. I can order my folks not to be in contact with him, but I can't guarantee their compliance."

"What do we do now?" Guy asked.

"How long would he normally remain there?" Hastings asked Parker.

"Hard to say. Different kinds of waste get discarded in

different areas. If he just got there, it could be at least an hour."

"Didn't you say you could track his movements, well, those of the vehicle, for any given time?" Syd asked.

"Yeah," Parker replied.

Rick gave him the date of Kerimides's murder and Parker checked it out. "Yeah, looks like he, or the vehicle anyway, was there from midnight to two."

That data went a long way toward identifying Terry as the killer.

Parker, who didn't know the significance of what he'd just uncovered, entered more keys. "I asked it to track the vehicle's movements over the last hour."

Once again the three heads popped over his shoulders. Parker studied the data when the report appeared. "Hmm. It's already been there an hour."

He keyed in something else. "I changed the time frame to the last two hours." They all waited for the next report. "Looks like the vehicle got there ninety minutes ago."

"This isn't good," Hastings said, more to himself than the other three. He pulled out his phone. "Quinn? Hastings. We may have ID'd a key suspect in the Kerimides case."

He walked out of the office as he finished the call. His demeanor had changed when he returned, as if his face could look any sterner. "Since I don't have my vehicle, I need you to drive me to the site, where I'll meet up with the sheriff's people. It's time for you two to hold back and let us handle this part, because it could be dangerous if Terry is still there."

He handed Parker his card. "Call me if you learn Terry has moved on."

Syd drove them to the landfill.

Meanwhile, Beau took a call from Marianne.

Chapter Twenty-Four

"Where are you?" Marianne asked.

"Just leaving Torrance Waste Management. Terry hasn't shown up. His manager had a tracker on his vehicle for reasons I'll explain later. His vehicle has been parked at that hazardous waste landfill on the outskirts of town for some time. He may or may not still be there. It's likely he's our killer, although we still don't know why."

"I think I do," Marianne replied. "That's why I was checking in. I've been on the phone with Dr. Jenz Kobart, one of my old chemistry professors. After I described the extra chemicals and other products we found in the embalming room, he speculated that Kerimides was selling them off to parties who couldn't readily obtain them without drawing attention. In fact, he had an amazing theory ..."

"Sorry, hon. We'll catch up later. Hastings wants to talk to us right now."

He hung up.

She tried to call him back and got a busy signal. Didn't he realize the importance of what she'd learned? Disappointment flooded her body. *Suck it up, Marianne. You're a grown woman.* What had been so important that her own husband had cut her off?

Her first inclination was to stop and grab a caramel macchiato to salve her wounded ego. But she needed to hook up with Beau and the others as soon as possible so they had some idea what they might be walking into. If what Dr. Kobart had theorized was true, this Terry could be even more dangerous than a killer, which was already bad.

She'd never been to the hazardous waste landfill. She'd intentionally avoided it in case there were clouds of bacteria or whatever circling the area. Although she had a rough idea where it was located, she stopped the car long enough to activate her GPS.

Fifteen minutes away. Maybe she could meet up with Beau and the other two before they tried to corner that guy.

Her GPS took her through an older suburban area of town, then a few older farms that no longer seemed to be in operation and then into a deserted area of countryside. So deserted she didn't see any other vehicles, but the screen said she still had two miles to go.

Maybe she should pull over here and wait for Beau and company to catch up. She stopped long enough to call Beau again to let him know she was on her way. Still busy.

Everything she'd learned thus far in her PI intern class plus every bit of her own better judgment told her to stay where she was and wait to hear from Beau or one of the others. On the other hand, her beloved Beau might be walking into something he wasn't prepared to handle. She'd dealt with more killers than he had.

She'd go a little farther. Maybe Beau, Syd and Hastings were already there.

She drove another mile. Halfway. Seemed safe enough. Still no sign of anyone and just empty fields around her.

Beau had said they were on their way to the landfill, hadn't he? Was there another one somewhere else?

Why wasn't he returning her calls? Had something already happened to him?

Hold up. If he was in trouble, what could she do?

She called Rick. No answer from him either. What was going on? Had everyone else gone incommunicado?

Next she called Kat.

"What's up?" Kat asked. "Have they found Brewster's phone? I took some time off the case to check in at Lombardi's. I've been busy going over menu choices for summer. My new chef hates watermelon even though it goes so well in summer salads and looks nice on the table."

"Rick texted me a while back," Marianne said. "They found the phone. And instead of handing it over to Martinez immediately, like Micki and I did, they read off just enough recent text exchanges between Kerimides and Brewster for Brewster to come clean. You won't believe this. They were having an affair."

"No! You and Micki really should've made Martinez let you read Kerimides's phone. Then you would've been the first to know," Kat said.

"But she apparently was due over at Brewster's place so she could serve the warrant. At least I've got some new info of my own." She ran Professor Kobart's idea past Kat to get her reaction.

"It's all coming together, isn't it?" Kat said.

"That's why I called. Have you been in touch with any of the others? Apparently they think they've tracked down the guy who's been picking up the funeral home's waste plus whatever Kerimides was selling to him at the hazardous waste landfill. Beau, Syd and Hastings are on their way there now. Plus, I suspect Rick, Trip, Guy and Martinez are meeting them. I can't reach either my husband or Rick."

"And you're on your way as well?"

"Sort of. I'm about a mile away. I haven't seen any of them. I must've gotten here first."

"You're not going alone?" Kat's voice rose. "You know that's a bad idea."

"Of course I do. I've had my fill of being locked in doggie spas and inside old fridges. But I'm worried about Beau. He hung up on me before I had time to tell him about Professor Kobart's suspicions. I thought maybe if I got just a little closer ..."

"Marianne!" Now Kat was screaming, totally out of character for her serene friend.

"I know, I know. But this is new territory for Beau. Sort of." Okay, he'd been trapped in the doggie shampooing stall along with her when a hurricane was bearing down on the town. But he still was unprepared to deal with a killer.

"Maybe Rick will pick up when he sees my number. I'll try calling him, and if I learn anything more, I'll call you back."

"Okay. Thanks."

Kat had only reinforced Marianne's own qualms about proceeding on her own. But Kat wasn't saddled with her overactive imagination, the same one that kept her writing one-act plays. Sitting here now with nothing to do but wait to hear from Beau, all her mind could picture was a gun trained on Beau and the others while Terry prepared his getaway.

If they'd all walked into a trap, perhaps she could shake things up by appearing on the scene to get them out of Terry's clutches.

She took the last mile at ten miles an hour. No sign of any vehicles, even as she came to the entrance. She couldn't help noticing numerous warning signs along the way and especially as she reached the entrance. A high metal fence prevented her from seeing much inside until she arrived at the entrance, a wide gate that was open. With all the signs keeping intruders out, the gate wouldn't be open unless they'd arrived and driven in.

She cocked her head. Had she heard something? A bird maybe. Or a gunshot? No, probably not. Probably?

She should probably wait here and let the others confront Terry.

Then she thought she heard it again, whatever it was.

Her fight or flight instincts, which she only heard about in theory in class, kicked in. They really did exist. She took her foot off the brake and drove slowly into the landfill.

She was surrounded by rows and rows of barrels on each side, blue to the right and red to the left. The road ascended a hill. Only after she'd come over the ridge did she see the two cargo vans, the one in back white with black lettering that said Torrance Waste Disposal, and the one in front black. She couldn't make out much more. Where were Syd and Rick's cars?"

For some reason, they hadn't yet arrived.

Best she turn around and get out of there.

But as she was attempting to make the turn, her door was thrown open and a hand holding a gun came through. "Sorry, lady, this area is off-limits."

"So I noticed," she tried to say, stumbling over her words. "I'll take off and leave you alone."

"That wouldn't be wise."

He looked like her idea of a mountain man. Well over six feet, his black hair shaggy and long, he wore a pair of black overalls over a dirty tan, long-sleeved knit shirt. His face was pockmarked. How any of this sunk in, she'd never know, as scared as she was. Her hands had locked on the steering wheel as she tried to breathe a normal breath.

His long, muscular arm reached in and turned off the car. "Get out."

"Wh-what are you doing?" she asked before realizing how inane that sounded.

"That's my question for you," he returned. "No one comes in here unless they're hauling waste."

She reached for the first response she could come up with. "I, uh, got lost."

"What were you looking for, hell?" He laughed at his own joke, his voice close to what she imagined the devil himself might sound like.

"Please, put the gun down. I mean you no harm," she said as calmly as her trembling voice would allow.

"Get out of the car," the man ordered. "You'll be sorry if I have to repeat myself again."

Why hadn't she thought to call someone, anyone, and keep her phone on before he got to her? She had no choice now but to stumble out of the car, leaving behind her purse and everything else that might save her.

"What's this?" asked a second male voice appearing from nowhere.

"Claims she got lost," the first man said. "Hard to believe with all those signs out there warning folks off. You a reporter, lady?"

"N-no," she replied. "I told you, I made the wrong turn. Please let me back in my car. I'll leave immediately."

"Get rid of her, Terry," the other man snarled. He wore a one-piece, dark green uniform with a name tag that said, "Jed, S.S. Landfill."

"I'm not taking on another murder charge," the man named Terry said.

"Then tie her up or something. We've gotta get out of here."

Terry had the second guy hold the gun on her while he returned to his vehicle. He was back in a minute with a coil of rope and a dirty rag.

"Turn around," Terry ordered. The second guy helped the first wrap the rope around her, finishing by tying her hands together. Terry made her open her mouth long enough to insert the rag.

She almost passed out from the acrid taste. She tried not to breathe in the fumes, but her lungs had a mind of their own.

The men dragged her to the space between the two vans and forced her to lean against the front of the white van. The back of the black van was open, revealing a small counter near the front surrounded by the same waste canisters she'd observed in Kerimides's embalming room, what appeared to be test tubes in a holder and two open cardboard boxes. One said "syringes" and the other said "vials."

She and Professor Kobart had guessed correctly. Although at this moment that realization gave her little comfort. She'd interrupted the production of what appeared to be fake drugs, most likely the weight-loss kind.

These two wouldn't let her go since she was witnessing their handoff. She needed a miracle to get out of here.

Where were Beau and the others? They should've been here long before she arrived.

As if in answer to her thoughts, a voice barked over a bullhorn. "This is the sheriff, Terry. Step away from your vehicles and lay down your guns."

In answer, Terry pulled Marianne into his arms, his gun trained on her, while the one named Jed took off running away from the sound

"Got a hostage, here, Sheriff. She's not getting out of here alive if you don't let us go."

"Let her go. You're surrounded."

Terry yanked her farther away from his van so whoever was out there could see her.

She tried to recall the class on self-defense. Her arms and mouth might be immobilized, but her legs and feet were still free. She had one chance. It was risky. Terry could shoot her if she made any attempt at escape.

But since the voice on the bullhorn was Quinn, that meant he was there with his team. Beau and the others might not be there yet, but the professionals had made it.

She couldn't see them, but they had to be near.

She gauged her surroundings and her captor. Now or never.

She kicked back with as much fury as she could muster, attempted to duck and waited for the worst.

"Yow!" Terry cried, releasing her to pat down wherever her foot had landed and letting her fall forward.

She heard movement, and brown uniform legs surrounded her and Terry.

"Hands behind your back," Quinn said to Terry.

"Got him, Sheriff," another voice called from the direction Jed had run. "Claims he's the guard at the entrance."

"Cuff him, anyhow," Quinn shouted back.

Meanwhile, the rag was pulled from her mouth and someone began removing the rope.

"Are you okay, Mrs. Putnam?" It was Deputy Martinez.

"Much better than a minute ago," Marianne breathed unsteadily. "Is Beau here?"

"The sheriff held him back until we could get those two in custody and make sure you're all right."

"Marianne!" Beau cried, swooping down on her. "Why in the world are you here? By yourself?"

"I thought you were in danger," she answered lamely.

"Me? Quinn made Syd and me stay in his car once we got here. The same for Rick, Guy and Trip. We're parked on a side road where those two couldn't see us. Then one of the deputies spotted you, and best-laid plans fell apart."

Rick was there within a minute. "Marianne? Are you okay?"

"I will be. As soon as I can get the taste of that awful rag out of my mouth."

Rick sent someone off to find water for her.

"I'm sorry, Rick," she said. "I knew I shouldn't follow them on my own, but I thought Beau was in trouble. And they spotted me before I could get turned around."

"Guess I can skip the lecture, then," he replied. "You're

already harder on yourself than I could be. And I'm sure you haven't heard the last from Beau," he added as an afterthought.

"I figured out what they were up to," she said in a weak attempt to redeem herself.

"Yeah, Kat texted me. You need to get back to her as soon as you can. She's been very worried. I have to check in with Quinn."

"I'm sorry, Beau. That doesn't begin to cover how stupid it was for me to come in here on my own when I know better. But I was worried about you. That you'd gotten yourself into a fix you couldn't get out of. Ironic, huh?"

He held her by her upper arms and stared into her eyes, as if trying to assess her mental state. "They made all of us non-pros stay back while Quinn and his army charged the scene. I had no idea you were here until a minute ago when one of the deputies told me. How did you not notice us?"

"I didn't see any other roads but this."

"They said Terry was holding you hostage."

"Not for long. I used one of the techniques we learned in self-defense."

His eyebrows went up in surprise. "You got yourself loose?"

"Well ... no. But my kick was enough to throw him off balance so the deputies could take him down."

"Quinn wants us to clear out of here so his team can process the scene. Rick told me to get you and head over to Kat's place, where we can debrief."

She didn't object, even though clearly Rick didn't want her moving around on her own, here or wherever.

While Rick stayed behind to confer with Quinn and his

people, Beau and Marianne headed to Syd's car. Only as she put space behind herself and her recent close call with death did it dawn on her that they'd accomplished their goal. "We did it, Beau!" she cried as relief surged through her limbs. "We caught the killer."

Chapter Twenty-Five

Kat was waiting for them when Marianne, Beau, Syd and Trip arrived at her house. She immediately folded Marianne into her arms. "I've been so worried since I last talked to you."

The other three took off to graze on the feast Greta had put together for them.

"I'm sorry I worried you," Marianne replied. "Guess that's all I'll be saying the rest of the evening. Or maybe the rest of our training, if I haven't already spoiled that."

"Nonsense," Micki said, arriving with Guy and Rick. "You took the initiative, my friend. That sometimes comes with risks, but you managed to throw that killer off guard enough for the law to take him and his buddy down."

"Gather round, everyone," Rick called. "Let's hold off taking advantage of the snack feast Greta prepared. We need to process what just happened as soon as possible. Before we have to give Quinn the official version." He turned to Marianne. "Do you need more water?"

The taste from that oily rag still lingered in her throat. She'd found a mint in her purse, but sucking it wasn't helping. But there was no way she wanted to worry the others, particularly Beau. "No, thanks. I'm fine." She let Beau lead her over to the love seat.

"Congratulations, everyone," Rick began. "The killer has been caught."

"What?" Guy asked.

"Thanks to Marianne and Micki's discovery of the extra chemicals, solutions and waste containers in the funeral home's embalming room, Marianne and an old chemistry prof figured out where they were going and how they were being used."

"That's what you were doing in the middle of that land-fill?" Trip asked.

"Well, no. I had no idea that Terry was meeting his cohort there. Beau told me that you guys were headed to the landfill to question Terry because he was late returning from his drop-offs. I was there looking for you all. Who was the other guy?"

"Quinn is still tracking down that information," Rick said. "It looks like he was the handoff guy for a small group producing and selling a fake weight-loss drug. In other words, my friends, team, we not only got the murderer, we helped take down a nasty black-market operation. We did good for our first time out."

"And we're not even certified PI interns yet," Micki crowed.

"This didn't go perfectly," Rick said, "but we proved our value to the sheriff's team. In the days to come, we'll decon-struct our actions, learn from them and plan for the future."

"Do we know yet why Terry killed Kerimides?" Kat asked.

"We have an idea," Trip said, "based on what we learned

from Tad Brewster. We all know by now that he and Kerimides were lovers. Recently, Kerimides canceled several times he and Brewster were supposed to be together. We're conjecturing that Terry was pressuring him to increase the amount of chemicals he was getting for them, which Kerimides finally couldn't accommodate. Apparently he'd gotten in too deep to back out, so Terry killed him. Quinn and company are interviewing Brewster now along with Terry and the other thug."

"So Kerimides wasn't killed because of his objection to the dog park," Beau said.

"Most likely not," Rick replied. "We should know more about that once Brewster has been fully debriefed. The noise thing probably was a ruse. I'm guessing a dog park behind the funeral home would have brought too much attention to the rear entrance and Kerimides's dealings with Terry."

"That means the dog park proposal might actually go through," Marianne said, thinking of Solomon. "Brewster must've been against it as a favor to Kerimides, although he may change his mind now."

"And if he bows, Sheridan won't be far behind," Beau said.

"How soon can we give Solomon the good news?" Marianne asked.

"I've been debating whether to invite him to join us, since he's the one who got this rolling," Rick replied. "But in the end I decided to limit this gathering to us, at least for a bit. We all need time to process this success."

"Should we get out some champagne?" Kat asked.

"Not just yet," her fiancé responded. "I'd like to use the high we're all feeling to look into our future together. We had a lot of moving parts occurring simultaneously in this investigation, and we managed to keep them forging ahead without getting in each other's way."

"That worked thanks to your direction, Rick," Syd told him. "You knew when to send us off on our own and when to step in yourself."

"Thanks, Syd. That means a lot," Rick replied.

"Especially coming from the Queen of Control," Trip said, putting an arm around his wife.

"But looking ahead," Rick continued, "that may not always be the case with future cases. We may not need or want the sheriff's department to accompany us. Six of you will soon get your PI intern certificates. You'll each be able to handle more on your own so I can focus on securing other business or dealing with other cases."

"What are you saying, Rick?" Guy asked. "It almost sounds like you're having second thoughts about us all participating in the business."

"No, I didn't mean to give you that idea. I just want to make sure the commitment is still there. And if anyone has changed his or her mind, that's okay. This Kerimides thing has been a learning experience for all of us."

"What aren't you saying?" Micki asked.

"Leave it to you, my journalist friend, to keep digging. Okay, here's what's on my mind. Maybe it was working so close to the concept of death with the funeral home involved. Whatever, I started thinking more about my own mortality. My other contemporaries are spending more time with grandchildren, traveling around the world or learning new skills or hobbies. I've made the decision to take on a whole new career, go into business when I've always worked for some form of government.

"And Katrina, you've not only begun a singing career, you've taken on the challenge of running a restaurant and making the ranch operational. As best I can tell, you're at peace with those decisions.

"But the rest of you, you could be living the high life of retirees. If you find going forward that this isn't how you want to spend the next years of your lives, I'll understand. I'm not suggesting you dabble, but you know what I'm saying."

"Thank you for your candor, man," Trip said. "Beau and I haven't given up playing golf a couple times a week. And the women? My wife is into her interior design projects. And Micki ..."

"Is still helping me draft legislation to make work arrangements like ours, senior sleuths helping law enforcement, happen," Guy said.

"And don't forget the event we've all been waiting for is fast approaching," Micki said.

"Our graduation?" Kat said jokingly.

"Don't play with me, Katrina Faulkner," Micki replied. "There's a wedding on the horizon, graduation, new business or not."

Rick gazed at Kat. "No, I haven't forgotten. We've all got a lot on our plate. And now that I've had my say, time for that champagne."

Epilogue

Once the others left, Kat and Rick settled in for a light supper before he took off to meet with Quinn. Kat toyed with her salad while Rick devoured a roast beef sandwich. Although she was also hungry, some of his earlier comments concerned her. "Why did you bring up the subject of aging with the others?"

Rick took a last bite of sandwich and then wiped his mouth with a napkin. "I didn't come off too strong, did I? I didn't mean to, but the contrast between the six of us stuck behind the front lines at that landfill and Quinn and company engaging those two con artists caused me to question the future of Formero Investigations."

She attempted to get her mind around this. "You mean having to take a back seat to Quinn and others you once trained and led?"

"I hadn't quite thought of it that way, but yes, that's a good assessment. When I was sheriff, even though I'd started letting my team do the confrontational aspects of the job, I was still there at the rear calling the shots. Today's experience drove home the fact I'm no longer their commander."

It had been almost a year since he lost the election, and he was still dwelling on what he'd lost. She should have expected this, but the subject hadn't surfaced for a while. It concerned her that it still lay there just below the surface.

"Quinn and his folks wouldn't have been there had it not been for what you and the rest of us uncovered in our investigation," she said.

"That's what I've been running through my head. This first case has shown me I'm winding up with a different model of a PI business than what I thought I was getting when I first decided to pursue this path. Instead of one or two young Turks out to make a name for themselves, I've got six seniors with brains, experience and a desire to give back after long lives of success in other fields. Plus my very own attorney whenever we need some legal advice. I'm blessed in ways I never anticipated."

"Then you're not worried about what lies ahead?" she asked.

"Not in the least. But I do have to rethink how I want this organization to run, especially setting up a viable revenue-producing plan. We accepted this case from Solomon Ridgedale just for expenses, since we weren't entirely official yet. But we can't afford to do that from here on. All eight of us need to be paid."

"I don't ..."

"Yes, you do need to be paid."

"Maybe we can work out some sort of stock ownership plan," she suggested.

He made his index finger into a gun. "Bingo. We're traveling the same wavelength. Think I'll make an appointment with our ex-banker friend, Trip, to see what kind of plan we can devise."

THE NEXT AFTERNOON, the group was summoned back to Kat's for an update from Sheriff Quinn. "Deputies Hastings and Martinez have been grilling the cast of characters involved in this murder since yesterday afternoon. Thought you'd like to know what we've got so far."

"That's very generous of you, Brian," Rick replied. "We turned the case over to you and your people before tying up some loose ends. Hope you're here to humor our curiosities."

"I'll tell you what I can. Some points are still unresolved, so I won't go into those." He glanced over those gathered. "What I tell you isn't for publication, understood?"

Everyone nodded.

"First, we'd all like to hear from Mrs. Putnam, since she's the one who got us started looking into the counterfeit drug," the sheriff said, eyeing Marianne. "Please tell us how you came to that conclusion."

"Call me Marianne," she replied. "After Micki, Micki Demetrius, and I were shown the embalming room by Stacia Kerimides, we took a walk to come down from the experience. I made an offhand comment about needing to exercise more so I wouldn't have to take some weight-loss drug. That got me thinking. When Stacia pointed out the extra chemicals in the embalming room, she commented about how overstocking was so out of character for her brother-in-law. Recalling her statement, I wondered if those extra chemicals might have been used to concoct a black market version of the real thing? I'd heard the drug was quite expensive. Supposing someone had found a way to produce a less expensive version?

"I contacted my old chem professor, Jenz Kobart, to sound him out on that idea. I've never taken a weight-loss drug, the kind you inject yourself with, so I needed an expert opinion. Apparently if you look at one of those injection pens, the solution inside is basically colorless. This next part may be too much information, but it's important that we have some basic understanding of how someone was able to produce a counterfeit version of this class of drugs. According to Professor Kobart, the main active ingredient in most of these drugs is a GLP-1 receptor called semaglutide, which helps regulate blood sugar and appetite. Because it is a synthetic peptide, which is a short string of amino acids, it can only be produced under pharmaceutical conditions, which are highly controlled. It is mixed with other inactive ingredients, which keep it stable. Those include disodium phosphate dihydrate, sodium chloride, hydrochloric acid or sodium hydroxide and water.

"The two of us theorized that Gordon Kerimides was selling these chemicals to Terry and company whenever Terry picked up the legitimate waste materials. Terry and his cohorts then must have added those to their fake pens and sold them to people who couldn't afford the legitimate products.

"That's what they were doing on-site at the landfill yesterday. Apparently there isn't much traffic there at certain times of the day, so they felt pretty safe assembling their product right there amongst all that hazardous waste."

"You and your professor friend figured out about ninety-five percent of the operation," Quinn told Marianne and the rest of the group. "A few years back, Terry's brother, Nick, a chemist, was fired from one of the big pharmaceutical companies, which was just on the brink of releasing their weight-loss drug. Apparently he'd been working on a slightly different formula, which when perfected could produce a less expensive result. He believed his bosses got rid of him not only to eliminate dissention within the company but also smeared his name so he couldn't get a legitimate job elsewhere and thus help the competition.

"Nick Terry has been a man on a mission to prove his own product works by offering an experimental, off-market version to willing buyers, desperate overweight people who haven't been able to afford the legitimate versions. But because he's been unable to obtain some of the materials he needed, he turned to less than legal means to proceed. Bob Terry came on board anticipating a big payoff from the sales. Their cousin, Jed Larson, took the job at the landfill to ensure privacy for the production of the illegal product."

"They've been taking advantage of people who are probably desperate to lose weight," Syd said.

"Which is horrible," Kat added. "Has anyone gotten sick … or worse?"

"According to Bob Terry, all the buyers knew the chance they were taking. He claimed it isn't a counterfeit drug but at the moment just illegal because it hasn't been approved by the FDA."

"Have you arrested the brother yet?" Beau asked. "The chemist who started this whole thing."

"Brought him in last night, once Larson started talking. He's doing his best to disassociate himself from his brother and the murder charge. Claims he never realized his brother would stoop so low when Kerimides wanted out of the scheme. He thought someone connected with the proposed dog park murdered the man. His goal is to save lives, not take them. He also seems more than willing to tell his story. Sees himself as some sort of Robin Hood in the world of Big Pharma, the little guy trying to improve the lives of the overweight population."

"Why did Kerimides agree to supply Terry?" Guy asked. "The business appeared to be in good shape, and from what we've all learned about Kerimides's private life, he wasn't a big spender."

"My financial experts are just starting to unravel that part of the story along with input from Tad Brewster. He couldn't supply any hard evidence, but apparently Kerimides shared a lot of confidential information when they were ... together. Kerimides told him he'd been betting online, something to do in the hours he wasn't working on a client and Brewster was unavailable. He'd been paying off his losses by dipping into the business's funds only he had access to. We hope to get more details now that we know where to look on his computer and that burner phone you found."

"Do you think Tad Brewster was involved in the illegal weight-loss drug scheme?" Beau asked. "We didn't pick up any indication of that when Marianne and I interviewed him."

"We don't know yet. Brewster is being very forthcoming with us in hopes of keeping his affair with Kerimides out of public notice. It was his jealousy that prompted him to stake out the back entrance of the funeral home and actually witness Terry come and go the night Kerimides was murdered. He should've come forward immediately, but he was trying to cover up his involvement with the victim."

"We've already assumed Kerimides's objection to the proposed dog park didn't have anything to do with the potential noise," Marianne said. "That he was simply trying to draw attention away from the back entrance. Was that the case?"

"Most likely," Quinn replied. "But if he wasn't part of the black-market operation, Brewster must've truly believed the noise aspect."

"Or he just didn't question his lover," Rick said.

Maybe that meant Brewster could be convinced to change his mind about the dog park. Probably too soon to tell.

"Why kill him?" Syd asked. "Did Kerimides fall down on the job?"

"Terry isn't saying much about the murder," Quinn replied, "even though we've got him dead to rights. Not just with Brewster's eyewitness testimony, but we also found the same kind of wire in the van that was used to strangle Kerimides. And Terry's crony, Larson, is showing signs of turning on him about the murder in exchange for a reduced sentence. Have no fear. We've got the right culprit."

"Has Terry said anything about the dog collar?" Beau asked.

"Funny you should ask. When he was denying having anything to do with Kerimides's death, he said something about our needing to pay more attention to the people he was keeping from getting their dog park, adding, 'Why else would they choke him with a dog collar?' We've not released that detail to the public. Only you folks and my team would know that. Referring to the dog collar not only clinches him as the killer, but the fact he brought it with him takes the crime into first-degree territory."

"How soon can we let Solomon Ridgedale know all this?" Marianne asked.

"He probably knows already," Quinn said. "He called soon after we brought in Terry and Larson wanting to talk to either Hastings or Martinez." He scratched his head. "Someday I mean to identify the town's grapevine. It could save us days of tracking down criminals."

"Let us know when you find out," Micki said. "We might want to recruit the sources for our investigations."

"Speaking of which," Quinn continued, "if I haven't said so already, good job everyone, especially since it was your first time out as Formero Investigations. My two deputies, Pilar Martinez and Colin Hastings, spoke well of your contribution to solving this murder. That's a lot coming from them. They weren't sure how working with private citizens would turn out, but they've been impressed with your talents. I can't say how our interaction might go in the future, but we're willing to consider some sort of mutually acceptable arrangement."

"Thanks, Brian," Rick replied. "We look forward to whatever that interaction might entail."

Quinn rose. "That's where we are at the moment. Thanks again for your help."

MARIANNE SLEPT WELL THAT NIGHT, after meeting with Quinn. Sure, pieces of various lectures in her PI Intern class popped into her brain from time to time, but the dreams about the embalming room that she'd been having ever since overkilling her research of embalming rooms online went away. No more thoughts about hazardous waste containers.

With interviews for the Kerimides case ended and her next PI Intern class a week off, she had time to focus on her own life on this bright morning. As she showered, she considered drafting a new play, this one set in a funeral home. But when she sat down at her laptop, the premise didn't gel. Too soon. Her brain needed more time to clear.

Perhaps a walk would help her focus. Mortimer benefited. He tilted his head to the side as she put his leash on him as if to ask, "What's up with you?" Today he was content to walk near her side rather than his usual pattern of pulling ahead as much as his leash would allow, as if sensing her mood.

"Hey, wait up," a familiar male voice called from behind her.

Solomon Ridgedale and Daisy caught up. "I've been so tempted to call you since your email the other night but have held back just in case the Kerimides investigation was ongoing."

"I still can't tell you much, Solomon. The charges against the individuals involved are still pending." She proceeded to give him the headline version of the story, just a little more detail than the media was carrying.

"But you're sure you got the right man?" he pushed.

"I can't answer that for sure."

"But the heat's off me?"

"For all intents and purposes, yes."

"Good! Then maybe the council can proceed with the dog park," he said. "Rumor has it that the dead man's objections about noise bothering his mourners was a ruse just to take attention away from the back entrance."

"I can't confirm that officially," she returned, as much as she wanted to reveal the whole story to him, especially her part in it. "As for the council, Brewster and Sheridan might still disagree."

"But there's still one other vote."

"Avery Wallace? I suppose it's possible she'll support the proposal," Marianne said.

"More than," he said mysteriously.

She pulled up. "What are you implying?"

"While you guys were busy investigating, I made an appointment with Councilwoman Wallace to brief her on the proposal and fill in any gaps in her understanding of it."

"And she accepted?"

"That she did." He sounded proud of himself. "In fact, she asked if we could meet at her gallery. I told her that would be great, since I was a big art lover."

"I didn't know that."

"Nor did I until I found myself telling her I was. Spent several hours online memorizing her website."

Though Mortimer was yanking his leash, she wasn't ready to move on until she got the full 411 from Solomon. "Did it work?"

He returned a sheepish smile. "For about ten minutes until I got the artist of one mixed up with the title of another. Nonetheless, she was impressed with my effort. Enough to go out for a glass of wine with me. One drink, which turned into three." The sheepish expression from before morphed into one that reminded her of the Mona Lisa. She knew a little something about art too.

"Solomon! You're not suggesting ...?"

"The rest is private. Let's just say I'm pretty sure she'll vote yes."

"Congratulations, I guess?"

"Better yet, she likes Daisy."

He wanted her to ask how Avery had met his dog, but she stopped short of going there. She'd save that question for another time. He sounded a little too satisfied right now.

"It sounds like things are working out for you, and I'm happy for that."

"I wouldn't be in this position if it wasn't for you and Beau and your friends, Marianne. I can't begin to tell you how much I appreciate Rick for taking on my case. Gratis."

"Your case came as he was just starting his business and before the rest of us earned our credentials, or you'd be looking at a large bill right now." She said it jokingly, but she also wanted him to realize that he'd benefited from the fact they weren't yet established.

"About that? I want to do something to thank you all for clearing my name."

"Just give us a good review if you're ever asked," she said, knowing the road ahead for Formero Investigations wouldn't necessarily run smooth for some time.

"Of course. But I haven't given up on showing you some sign of my appreciation. You still have no idea what you all did for me."

TWO WEEKS LATER, Marianne along with Micki and Syd were summoned by Kat to her ranch house.

"Why are we here?" a somewhat huffy Syd asked Kat. "I told you the great room isn't quite finished. I'd rather it remain off-limits until it is."

Kat touched her shoulder. "Not to worry. Even I haven't peeked through that temporary screen you put up. Your efforts are still all your own. Instead, I want you all to follow me to the game room."

"The game room?" Syd asked. "I haven't gotten anywhere near it yet." She sounded panicked, for Syd.

"I don't recall asking you to do it, Syd," Kat replied. "Maybe down the road you can tackle it, but for now I'm happy with the pool, ping-pong and game tables and the bar. However, there's one new addition I wanted you all to see as soon as possible."

"You bought furniture you didn't tell me about?" Syd cried.

"Not exactly. And I didn't purchase it."

At the entrance to the game room, she stepped aside. "Ta-da!"

"Is that what I think it is?" Marianne asked, holding back, afraid she was seeing a mirage.

"Come and see for yourselves," Kat said, inviting them all to join her at the square table that stood across the room.

"This is one of those automatic mah jongg tables like Bitsy's!" Micki said, making a beeline to the room's new addition.

"That's right," Kat answered. "If it's okay with you all, for now we'll keep it here at the ranch house until we find it a permanent home. There's a huge selection of whiskeys, gin, vodka, et cetera over at the bar that has been gifted to the guys."

"We were just kidding about your buying one of these," Marianne said, touching the outside edge of the table. "But I'm glad you did."

"Actually, I didn't buy it. It's a gift from Solomon Ridgedale. We didn't charge him for our investigative services, since the Kerimides case was like a practice run. But he wanted to do something to show his appreciation, and Rick suggested this for us and additions to the bar for the guys."

"How did Rick know we wanted one of these?" Syd asked.

"He asked me for ideas, and this was the first thing that came to mind. I suppose I could've asked for something else if I'd put my mind to it ..."

"No way! This was the perfect way for him to say thank you," Marianne said, recalling her conversation with Solomon the day after they helped the sheriff bring in Terry. She debated whether to share how he had connected with Avery Wallace but decided that was more a wait-and-see situation. Instead, she pulled out a chair and settled in. "Who's ready to play?"

"I'm in," Syd said, her earlier miff having disappeared. "Good thing I always have my card in my purse."

"I have extras in case anyone else needs one," Kat said.

"I'm fine," Marianne said.

"Me, too," Micki added.

"Then let's get started," Kat said. "We probably won't have much free time in the days ahead as we finish our PI Intern course and settle into working for Formero Investigations."

"And continue planning your wedding," Micki reminded her.

Kat chuckled. "Yes, of course our wedding. But I'm confident the planning is in good hands."

"We're in position. All you need to do is decide on your dress, the flowers, meal and invite list," Micki said.

"As soon as we finish our course, I promise to give those items my full attention," Kat replied. "Other than helping Rick continue to set up the business."

"Let us take over that part," Syd told her. "I'm almost finished with the great room, and then I'll be available. Trip could help Rick now."

"And Guy, too," Micki added. "Since he's not involved in the course."

"Okay, okay. Thanks, you guys."

As the conversation lulled, Micki spoke up. "Hey! Are we going to play mah jongg or not?"

"Right!" the other three chimed in.

"Are we sworn to secrecy about this?" Micki asked. "If not, you'll be swamped with requests for our group to play here."

"I suggest we keep this gift to ourselves for a while so it doesn't look like we're trying to outdo Bitsy," Kat said.

"Oh, right," Micki said.

Kat pushed a few buttons on the center control, and four walls of thirty-six tiles each popped up for each player.

"Two bam," Marianne, the first to play, said after the preliminary exchange of tiles was finished.

"Six dot," Syd said, discarding her tile.

"Nine bam," Micki said.

"Seven dot," Kat said.

"Take," Marianne called out. She took the seven dot and placed it with two others on her rack to make a pung, three of a kind.

It went on like that for a few more minutes while Marianne proceeded to place a pung of green dragons on her rack and then a pung of seven dots. "Mah jongg!" she pronounced excitedly when Syd discarded a Flower. She then placed another pung of sevens, this time seven craks, and added a flower to the one she'd just picked up. "See. It's the third down on 'Any Like Number.'"

"Good try, but I'm afraid your hand is dead," Syd told her.

"No, it's two Flowers, any three suits and any dragon," Marianne replied.

"That it is," Kat agreed. "But it's a concealed hand. You can't put anything on the rack until you have the full hand."

Marianne checked her mah jongg card. "Oh. I didn't think we had to pay attention to those unless we were playing for money, which today we aren't."

With a dead hand, Marianne sat out the rest of the game while the other three played with the remaining tiles. At length, Micki won with a Consecutive Run hand of craks, two ones, three two craks, four three craks, three four craks, and two five craks.

"Congratulations, Micki, you won our inaugural game," Marianne said. "I won't forget about concealed hands again."

A few minutes later, Marianne had just called "mah jongg" when her phone beeped. "Looks like I just received a text from Solomon Ridgedale." She pulled it up before anyone could object. "This is intended for all of us."

Marianne and the rest of you: I've just come from the latest council meeting. They approved the dog park proposal five to zero! Even Brewster changed his mind. It'll be some time before Daisy can enjoy running free in

*the new dog park, but it never would have happened
without your help.*

*By now you are probably aware of the small tokens of my
appreciation I sent you. My sources tell me you are already
enjoying your automatic mah jongg table. Hope you have
discovered the hidden cupholders, just perfect for holding a
flute of champagne from the stash I sent to the men in your
entourage. I asked Rick to put a bottle of bubbly on ice.
Why not open one now and celebrate the successful conclusion of the Kerimides case and the start of your new
venture?*

About that time, Rick, followed by Trip, Beau and Guy,
entered the room.

"Just received word from Solomon that it's time for champagne," Rick said. "I was planning to do something similar,
but we'll let him take credit for the idea."

He headed over to the bar and lifted a stainless-steel
bucket holding two bottles of champagne onto the bar top.
Meanwhile, Trip brought up a tray of champagne flutes.
While he filled them from the now open bottles, Beau and
Guy served the four women.

Once everyone had a glass, Rick lifted his in a toast. "It's
no coincidence that we hold our glasses high around this
mah jongg table. Mah jongg is what brought you four women
together a while back and where you started your first investigation. Over time, you guys came on board. And now, here
we are, about to embark on a brand-new adventure. Thank
you all for signing on."

"To Formero Investigations!" Trip said.

"Aye, aye," the rest called out.

"And to Solomon Ridgedale and the energy-filled Daisy," Marianne added. "Formero Investigations would have launched soon anyway, but it was my fateful walk with our granddog, Mortimer, where I ran into him and Daisy, that got us started."

They all clinked glasses, sipped their champagne, and Formero Investigations was off and running.

Dear Reader,

Thank you for reading this book. If you liked it, won't you please take a minute to leave a review?

This is my first cozy mystery series. After I published Book 9 in the Mah Jongg Mystery series, *Courtesy Call,* I took a four-year break to write seven books in the Nailed It Home Reno Mystery series and three books in the Unscripted Detective Mystery series. You can learn more about them and also the eleven contemporary romances I've published on my website, www.barbarabarrettbooks.com.

To keep up with all three of my cozy mystery series, sign up for my newsletter at https://www.subscribepage.com/BBCozies.

Follow me on Facebook: http://bit.ly/2aXZvG9
Follow me on Bluesky: bbarrettauthor.bsky.social

Fondly,
Barbara

Excerpt of Book 11 in the Mah Jongg Mystery series, *Off the Rack*, to be released in the late fall of 2025 or early 2026.

A week and a half later, the six PI intern candidates sat around Kat's living room studying for their final final.

"Can you all believe we've reached this point?" Kat asked the others.

"We should do something to celebrate once we've all received that little piece of paper," Beau said.

"Throwing a big-time wedding doesn't count?" his wife joked.

"Well, there is that, but no offense, Kat, but I meant something where we are all the stars," Beau replied.

"No offense taken," Kat said. "What did you have in mind, Beau?"

"I don't know. Probably not a party. The wedding will take care of that. Perhaps a trip? Yeah, how about we take a short cruise? We should take advantage of living here in Florida."

Micki was about to list all the reasons why that was a bad

idea when Greta appeared at the door. "Kat? Ms. Faulkner? There's someone here to see you."

"That's okay, I'll announce myself, said a female voice behind her.

An unfamiliar sheriff's department deputy stepped around Greta. "I'm Deputy Paloma Callahan. Sheriff Quinn was called away on a family matter, so he sent me. Which one of you is Katrina Faulkner?"

"That would be me," Kat said, rising and coming over to her. "What's up, Deputy?"

"Have you been doing business with a woman by the name of Georgia Julienne?"

"Yes. She's designed my wedding dress."

"Wedding dress. Yes, uh, we found your name with it. I'm afraid I must inform you that the dress has been involved in foul play. Ms. Julienne has been murdered."

Acknowledgments

This book would not have been possible without the input and suggestions of my editor, Chris Kridler, of Sky Diary Productions. Chris also produced the incredible cover, formatted the manuscript and enhanced the back cover blurb.

Thanks also to Sharleen Newton, Harriet Sawyer and Bernadine Marsis for their keen proofing eyes.

As always, thanks to my husband, Veryl, for his ongoing support.

BOOKS BY BARBARA BARRETT

Cozy Mysteries

The Mah Jongg Mystery Series

Craks in a Marriage

Bamboozled

Connect the Dots

Beware the East Wind

Flower Power

Jokers Wild

The Charleston Challenge

The Dragon Lady Gets Her Due

Courtesy Call

Back Against the Wall

also available in paperback

Nailed It Home Reno Mysteries

Measure Twice, Murder Once

Loose Screw

Death by Drywall

Homicide by Hammer

Nuts and Bolts

Snared by the Snake

Wrenched at the Reindeer Run

A LITTLE ABOUT
BARBARA BARRETT

BARBARA BARRETT started reading mysteries when she was pregnant with her first child to keep her mind off things like her changing body and food cravings. When she'd devoured as many Agatha Christies as she could find, she branched out to English village cozies and Ellery Queen.

Later, to avoid a midlife crisis, she began writing fiction at night when she wasn't at her day job in human resources for Iowa State Government. After releasing eleven full-length romance novels and two novellas, she returned to the cozy mystery genre, using one of her retirement pastimes, the game of mah jongg, as her inspiration. Not only has it been a great social outlet, it has also helped keep her mind active when not writing.

The Mah Jongg Mystery series is her first venture into writing cozy mysteries. After taking a short break from this series when the ninth book ended a few years ago, she now returns with Book 10, *Back Against the Wall*. Former Sheriff Rick Formero has left the public sector and is opening his own private investigation agency. The series still focuses on the four women friends and mah jongg players, but they are now joined by the men in their life, and they are all planning to be part of Formero Investigations.

Barbara has also published seven books in the Nailed It Home Reno mystery series and three books in the Unscripted Detective mystery series.

Barbara is a member of Sisters in Crime, SinC—Iowa, Twin Cities Sisters in Crime and Florida Star Fiction Writers.

She is married to the man she met her senior year of college. They have two grown children, eight grandchildren and three great grandchildren.

Now retired, she spends her time between Iowa and Minnesota. She earned her B.A. degree in History from the University of Iowa and her Master's Degree in History from Drake University.

When not in front of her laptop creating her next story, she plays mah jongg, travels and enjoys lunches with friends.

amazon.com/stores/Barbara-Barrett/author/B008WP39A8

bookbub.com/profile/barbara-barrett

bsky.app/profile/bbarrettauthor.bsky.social

instagram.com/barbarabarrett347

www.ingramcontent.com/pod-product-compliance
Lightning Source LLC
Chambersburg PA
CBHW071229210726
48293CB00002B/632